MURDER

BY THE HIDDEN BAY

Irish detectives scramble to find a killer

DAVID PEARSON

THE BOOK FOLKS

Paperback edition published by

The Book Folks

London, 2022

This book is a work of fiction. Names, characters, businesses, organizations, places and events are either the product of the author's imagination or are used fictitiously. Any resemblance to actual persons, living or dead, events or locales is entirely coincidental. The spelling is British English.

ISBN 978-1-80462-009-0

www.thebookfolks.com

MURDER BY THE HIDDEN BAY is the thirteenth standalone mystery in The Galway Homicides series. Details about the other titles can be found at the back of this book.

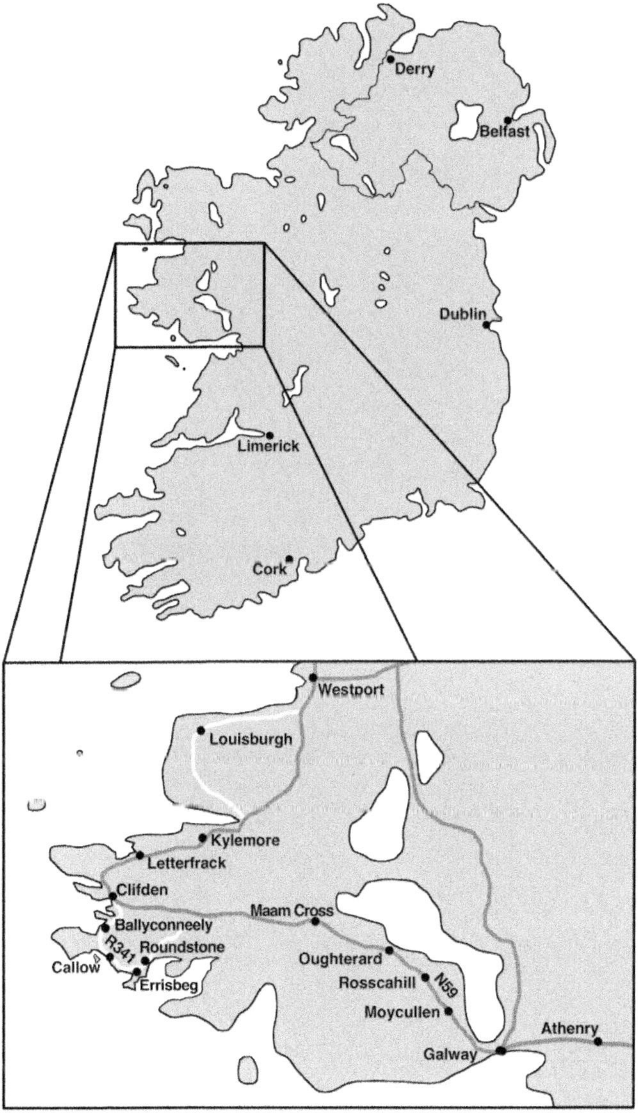

Derry
Belfast
Dublin
Limerick
Cork
Westport
Louisburgh
Kylemore
Letterfrack
Clifden
Maam Cross
Ballyconneely
R341
Roundstone
Callow
Errisbeg
Oughterard
Rosscahill
N59
Moycullen
Athenry
Galway

Chapter One

It was mid-September in the west of Ireland. The summer months had been kind to the place, with better than average weather and a resultant throng of tourists from all over Europe. The Wild Atlantic Way had been well publicised, and it had attracted visitors right through from Easter to the end of August. But now, with the kids having gone back to school, and the many holiday homes deserted again for the winter months, things in Roundstone had quietened down considerably.

The Bertraghboy Bay Hotel, just off the main street in the village on Monastery Road, had been busy throughout the holiday season. It was a modest establishment, with just fifteen bedrooms, but it featured an excellent dining room and a lively bar where people would assemble in the evening after a busy day walking or cycling around the area for the *craic*, as it was known. Several nights a week the proprietors employed a pair of traditional musicians to entertain their guests, and to draw others in from the surrounding hostelries, and it had worked well.

As is common in hotels of this size, many of the staff did several jobs. In the morning, during breakfast and afterwards when guests were checking out, staff would wait at table and act as receptionists. Then, when departing guests had left, the same staff would turn their attention to changing the bed linen and cleaning the rooms, and by the time that task was accomplished, the lunchtime trade would be starting. But the afternoons were usually very quiet, and that gave the busy personnel some respite before the place got going again at around six with more arrivals and of course the evening meal, and the bar.

Aoife Gilpin was one such staff member. She was a woman of twenty-three years who lived with her parents in a bungalow at the foot of Errisbeg. The house was unimaginatively named "Radharc na Farraige" which translated from Irish as "Seaview", and it did in fact live up to its name, having magnificent views out over the headland to the Atlantic Ocean, with the two white sandy beaches of Gurteen and Dog's Bay in between.

Aoife was industrious and pleasant with it, so she enjoyed year-round employment at the hotel, save for the month of January when it was closed for repairs and repainting. At that time, the owners would get away to the Canary Islands for their annual holiday, leaving the workmen to get on with it, and Aoife and the rest of the full-time staff with nothing to do for the month.

Aoife's day at the hotel started at half past seven in the morning. She would have preferred an hour later, but the French and German tourists in particular liked to make an early start, so breakfast service started at eight o'clock, and there were things to prepare before the guests arrived down.

Aoife travelled the three and a half kilometres from her home to the hotel by bicycle. She had a choice of two routes. She could cycle down along the R341 directly into the village, turning up Monastery Road to get to her destination, or she could travel on the more rural, narrower road known as Fuchsia Lane. It was a small road – more like a track really – before it reached the hotel and widened out to become Monastery Road. There was little or no difference in the distance involved, but the lane was quieter, often with no traffic at all at that early hour, and Aoife preferred it for that reason.

Aoife enjoyed her work at the hotel. Although the hours could be long, even taking into account the time that she had free in the afternoons, she enjoyed the company of the rest of the staff, and the variety of visitors that she encountered at the place, although the pay wasn't up to much, even when the tips were taken into account. The owners were fastidious in collecting all the tips and sharing them out evenly between everyone, so that at the end of the week Aoife often received as much as €50 on top of her wages. With few outgoings, although she did give her mother €100 a week towards the upkeep of the household, Aoife had accumulated quite a tidy sum in her post office savings account by the end of this particular summer.

It was a Thursday morning on that fateful day when Aoife set off for work as usual soon after seven. The sun was up, and there were just a few cotton wool clouds in the sky, so it looked as if it would be another beautiful autumn day in Roundstone as Aoife pedalled along Fuchsia Lane on her retro Dawes bicycle towards work. As she turned a bend in the road, she had to pull up sharply, as she encountered several black plastic sacks packed with rubbish or something across the thoroughfare, blocking her passage.

"God, who in their right mind has left those there?" she said to herself. She dismounted from her cycle, laying it down on its side on the grass verge, and went to remove the bags. She would shift them into the ditch, and maybe ask her father to come down later and take them away. Rubbish discarded like that gave a terrible impression to the tourists, and Aoife was very civic-minded in that regard.

As she stooped to lift the first of the bags from the road, she heard a noise behind her, and was just turning to see what was causing it, suspecting a rat or other scavenger, when she was hit hard over the head with such force that it was the last thing she ever knew. By the time she hit the ground, she was dead.

* * *

Pascal Brosnan ran the little Garda station at the edge of Roundstone village with his colleague, Mary Fallon. Fallon had joined the force just over a year ago from the training college at Templemore, and had originally been posted to Clifden. But Séan Mulholland, the sergeant in Clifden, not used to having females reporting to him, had reallocated Fallon to Roundstone, not knowing quite what to do with her. Fallon and Brosnan got on well together, and there was even a hint of some romantic involvement, but that was kept well under wraps and left entirely to speculation by anyone with an interest in the matter.

Fallon had left the station at six o'clock that Thursday evening as was her habit when there was nothing doing, but Brosnan had stayed on a bit to tidy up some papers and give the station a quick clean when, approaching seven, the phone rang. Normally, the phone would have been switched through to Brosnan's house at this hour, but as he was still there, he decided to answer it.

"Roundstone Gardaí," he said.

"Is that yourself, Pascal?" a woman's voice enquired.

"Yes, who's speaking please?"

"It's Brigid Gilpin here, Pascal, from Errisbeg. Listen, I'm a bit concerned about Aoife. She hasn't come home from the hotel, and I phoned them to see if she was working late or whatever, and they told me she hadn't turned in for work at all today. That's not like her, and I can't contact her on her mobile. I have her dinner here keeping warm on the stove."

"I see. Well could she have gone to visit a friend or something and just forgot to tell you? Or maybe there's no phone signal wherever she is."

"I telephoned her friends from the village, Pascal, and no one has seen her all day. It's not a bit like her, I tell you," Brigid Gilpin said.

"Mrs Gilpin, did Aoife take anything extra with her setting off for work this morning, like an extra bag or anything?"

"No. No, she left as usual at around seven. I gave her breakfast, and then off she went on her bicycle. God, I do hope nothing bad has happened to her. Help me, Pascal, won't you? Her father is beside himself with worry too."

"Where is Mr Gilpin just now, Mrs Gilpin?"

"He's gone out the road looking for her in his truck. He said he'd be back before it got proper dark."

"Right. Well, I'll start a few enquiries around and about, and don't worry, Mrs Gilpin, there's nearly always a perfectly ordinary explanation for these things. If you hear anything, let me know at once. My mobile number is 0816493004."

When Pascal Brosnan had finished the call with Aoife's anxious mother, he wasn't quite sure what to do. Should he call Sergeant Mulholland in Clifden and get his opinion on the matter, or should he just go down into the village and see if there was any news of the girl? Yes, that's what he would do, and he'd call in to the hotel along the way and see if there was any information to be gleaned from any of the rest of the staff. But he would keep it low-key. No point making a big fuss when the girl was probably safe and well in someone's house, or maybe she went into Galway to do some shopping and forgot to tell her mam.

As Brosnan moved around the town in the early evening, he thought he could observe a solemness that was not usual in the three pubs in the village. It was as if a cloud had descended upon the place. Word of the missing girl had spread in whispered chatter amongst the patrons, and there was much shaking of heads and tut-tutting going on, particularly from the older customers. Roundstone was not used to anything like this. It was a peaceful place. Oh, sure, from time to time a boisterous young man from the city would go a bit overboard with the drink and cause a rumpus, but Roundstone hadn't seen any real crime since Paddy the postman had been shot in an abortive raid on his van a few years back. But now, Brosnan could feel something in the air, and he didn't like it one little bit.

Chapter Two

Brosnan's enquiries of the previous evening had yielded nothing of interest concerning Aoife Gilpin. When Mary Fallon arrived at the station for work at nine o'clock, Brosnan filled her in on the story from the previous night, but held back on the strange atmosphere that he had sensed for fear she would think he was daft. He asked her what she thought they should do.

"God, I don't know, Pascal, it sounds a bit dodgy to me. Why don't you call the Gilpins' house and see if there's any news, and I'll telephone Sergeant Mulholland and put him in the picture?"

"Yes, perhaps you're right. There's nothing else much on anyway," Brosnan said rather dismissively, but in the back of his mind he had an increasingly uneasy feeling.

Mrs Gilpin told Pascal Brosnan that they had not heard from their daughter, and they were now very seriously concerned for her welfare.

"What are you going to do, Garda Brosnan? She's obviously a missing person. Are you going to organise a search team, or what, or do I need to call Clifden or Galway myself?" the woman said.

"No, Mrs Gilpin, you don't need to do anything. My colleague is on to Clifden right now about it, and we will start the missing persons procedure in a few minutes as soon as she has finished the call."

"I should hope so too," Mrs Gilpin said, and hung up the phone.

Brosnan could understand the woman's uncharacteristic curtness. He doubted if they had slept a wink last night, and these things had a habit of setting man and wife against each other.

Pascal Brosnan and Mary Fallon were discussing the situation. Séan Mulholland had advised Mary Fallon how to initiate the missing persons procedure, and he also said that he would advise the detective unit in Galway of the matter. Their first task was to get a recent photograph of the woman, copy it, and circulate it all around the village and the nearby homesteads. Then, they would contact the bus company that ran the only service from Roundstone to Galway a few times daily, and see if the driver had seen Aoife the previous day.

"Mary, will you go out to the Gilpins' house and see if you can get a decent photograph of her? I don't think I'm very popular with the mother just now," Brosnan said.

"Yes, sure. Do we need anything else while I'm there?" Fallon said.

"Well maybe if you could get a look in her bedroom without causing any further distress, that might be helpful."

"What am I looking for?"

"Anything that you think might be relevant. Letters, a laptop, CDs, that sort of thing, and get a feel for the place too. Try and get a picture in your mind of what Aoife is all about. And if you get a chance, ask her mother if she has a boyfriend, either past or present."

"Oh, OK. I hope I can handle it," Fallon said.

"Ah, you'll be grand. I have every faith in you," Brosnan said, smiling. He meant it too.

* * *

When Mary Fallon had departed on her mission and Pascal Brosnan was alone, an old man came into the Garda station.

The man was one of the local bachelors who lived close to the village in a modest cottage. He was a small man, with a weather-beaten complexion, dressed in an old brown tweed suit, with an open-necked shirt and a greasy cap perched on his head.

Brosnan got up and went to the counter.

"God, Pascal, I'm after finding a body up in the field. I'm not the better of it yet. The dog was getting a few sheep together for me, and he stopped at the thing. He never touched it, mind, but I had a look, and it's definitely someone all right. I just came straight here."

"All right, Festus," Brosnan said, recognising the man, "where exactly is this? Can you show me?"

"Sure, of course I can," Festus said.

Brosnan collected his peaked cap and jacket, locked the station making sure that the notice advising anyone concerned to call Clifden in an emergency was fixed to the door, and set off with Festus Rourke on foot towards Fuchsia Lane. The old man was not capable of walking briskly, so Pascal Brosnan stayed in step with him, feeling a little frustrated at the gentle pace. But after twelve minutes or so, they arrived at a rather rusty five-bar gate leading into an unkempt field where numerous dock weeds and rough grass sprouted. The old man pushed open the gate, allowing them to enter, and he led Brosnan up along the hedge to where the prone form of a young woman lay, face down, in the grass.

Brosnan's initial appraisal of the situation was that the girl was obviously dead, though he wasn't qualified to certify as such. But her dishevelled hair, and the remains of the overnight dew which had soaked the back of her coat, along with her ungainly posture left little doubt.

"Are you sure you didn't disturb her, Festus?"

"Oh, God, no. I only came in looking for a couple of my ewes, and that's when I saw her, poor thing. Do you think it's that lass that went missing yesterday?" Rourke said.

"And who told you about that, Festus?"

"'tis all over the village, Guard. But no one was expecting this!"

"Tell me, Festus, what time was it that you came in here and found her?"

"Ah now, Pascal, I'm not good with time. But I'd say about half an hour before I came into the Garda station."

"And what took you so long? After all, we have walked here in less than half that," Brosnan said.

"'twas the fright of it. I had to sit easy for a wee while to gather my breath. I've never seen a dead body before, not ever. And it fair took the wind out of me."

Brosnan could relate to the old man's story. The first time he had encountered a corpse in the line of duty, it had had much the same effect on him. It's not something you recover from easily.

Brosnan walked away from the old man and his gruesome find till he was out of earshot and called Mary Fallon.

"Mary, it's Pascal. Are you still at the house?"

"Yes. Mrs Gilpin is just getting a cup of tea for us. Why, what's up?"

Brosnan lowered his voice until it was barely a whisper.

"There's the body of a young woman in a field just off Fuchsia Lane. I'm here now with the man that found it. Don't say anything to the Gilpins just yet. We can't be sure it's her – but I doubt if it's anyone else. Stay there till you hear from me. I'm going to call Sergeant Mulholland now."

* * *

"Sergeant Mulholland, it's me, Pascal. I'm out here in a field off Fuchsia Lane near Roundstone village, and I've just found the body of a young woman here in the grass."

"Good God! Are you sure she's dead, Pascal?" Mulholland said.

"Yes, there's no doubt. Looks as if she has been here overnight. An old-timer found her when he went looking for a couple of sheep."

"Where's Mary?" Mulholland said.

"She's gone up to the Gilpins, but she hasn't said anything to them yet. She's just marking time."

"Right. Well, I'm on my way out there now. I'll bring Jim Dolan with me, and while we're travelling will you call Galway and see if you can speak to Inspector Lyons or Eamon Flynn and ask them to get Dr Dodd out too. You stay there and make sure the scene is preserved."

"What about the old guy?" Brosnan said.

"Let him off home, and ask him not to say anything till we get the people from Galway out at least. We don't want a bunch of onlookers. And tell Mary I'll call to the Gilpins as soon as we have confirmation of the woman's identity."

"Right, Sergeant. See you shortly."

Chapter Three

Senior Inspector Maureen Lyons was seated at her desk in Mill Street Garda station reading the Connaught Tribune. It was unusual for her to have time to read the newspaper, but things were quiet at the moment, so she felt no guilt at taking it easy for a few minutes whilst she nursed a cup of tepid instant coffee.

Her eyes fell on a photograph in the social and personal section of the paper where her life partner, Detective Superintendent Mick Hays, had been presented with a trophy for his sailing prowess at the annual regatta that had taken place in high summer. It was the yearly dinner, where prizes were handed out, and the sailing fraternity all sat down to a sumptuous meal. It had taken place in the Meyrick Hotel on Eyre Square, and there, grinning like a Cheshire cat, was her very own Hays looking resplendent in a dinner jacket and bow tie.

"God, you're a handsome devil, Mick Hays," Lyons said as she read the caption citing her beloved as the outright winner of the 28–33-foot solo class race from the Galway Bay Sailing Club's jetty out as far as Rosshill and back in July, when the sea was benign and the weather warm.

Her musing didn't last long. The phone on her desk jangled, disturbing her peace.

"Lyons," she answered, slightly vexed at the interruption.

"Hello, Inspector. It's Pascal Brosnan here from Roundstone." The man went on to describe the situation as briefly as he could.

"I see. OK, well I'll head out there immediately. I'll call Dr Dodd and Sinéad Loughran too and get them moving. Will you seal off the scene as best you can? Has Sergeant Mulholland been informed?" Lyons said.

"Oh, yes. He's on his way in now. He should be here in a few minutes. Mary is up with the Gilpins. Do you think we should say anything to them?"

"No, not yet at least. Wait till Séan gets there. He'll know how to handle it. I'll be with you in half an hour or so too."

"Right. I'll see you then."

As soon as Lyons had finished the call, she grabbed her jacket from the back of the chair and went out into the open plan office where the rest of the detective team sat.

"Sally, you're with me. We're off out to Roundstone. There's been a body found in a field. Eamon, can you call Dr Dodd and get Sinéad and himself moving. Sounds like we need the full forensic team and a black van. Pascal Brosnan can give you directions to the site," Lyons said walking briskly through the place towards the door.

"Right, boss. Do you want me out there too?" Eamon Flynn asked.

"No. You stay here and co-ordinate things for the moment. And could you let the superintendent know what's going on for me?"

"Yes, sure."

Detective Sergeant Sally Fahy was a pretty blonde woman in her late twenties. She had started her career with the police in Galway as a civilian worker, and had liked it so much that she applied for, and got, a job as a full-time member of the force. Early on, Maureen Lyons had recognised the woman's abilities for detection, and had made sure that she joined the team as soon as possible when she had completed her training. The two of them got on really well, and they had been through some tough scrapes together which had helped to build a strong and loyal bond between them.

The pair took Lyons' Volvo S60 for the journey which had been fitted with discreet blue lights and a siren that helped them cut through the morning traffic as they left the city bound for Connemara.

* * *

By the time Lyons had reached Oughterard, she spotted Sinéad Loughran's brightly coloured 4x4 and Dr Julian Dodd's shiny black Lexus falling in behind her Volvo, forming a convoy of sorts on their way to the grim scene.

"Any idea what this is all about, boss?" Fahy asked, as they left the town behind, crossing the bridge over the Owenriff River, and drove on past the old Sweeney's Hotel, before the road climbed steeply up onto the heathland.

"Not a clue, Sally. It's very unusual for there to be any serious crime in Roundstone. It's normally very quiet. Maybe the deceased is a tourist or something, though Pascal said that a local girl had been reported missing last night by her parents. God, I hope it's not her," Lyons said.

"Cripes, me too. How's Pascal handling it?"

"He's OK. Probably a bit shook, but he hides it well. But he will have his hands full when this gets out. The place will be deluged with press and probably TV as well."

They drove on apace across the bog. On either side of the road large ponds and lakes shimmered like silver in the morning sunlight, while the purple of the heather created a contrast to the greens and browns of the meagre covering of grass and reeds that lay on top of the rich peat deposits.

When they reached Roundstone, Lyons turned her car onto the narrow road that led away from the harbour, and passed the Bertraghboy Bay Hotel on her left, before stopping a few hundred metres further on.

Fuchsia Lane wasn't used to such traffic. The road was now completely blocked with other police vehicles. Lyons parked as close as she could manage to the gate that gave entry to the field, and got out.

Séan Mulholland had posted a uniformed officer at the entrance, who duly recorded their names, and allowed them in. Loughran and Dodd got busy erecting a plastic tent over the body that was still lying face down, and when this was accomplished, they entered to examine the scene. Lyons had the good sense to stand well back from them, as she waited patiently for news of the deceased.

Dr Julian Dodd was a man of about five foot seven inches in height. He was a very good pathologist, and his skills were recognised and appreciated by any of the Gardaí that had worked with him. But, possibly because of his somewhat diminutive stature, he often employed an ironic demeanour, and could be known from time to time to appear a little intolerant. After about ten minutes, Dodd, now dressed in a white one-piece paper scene-of-crime suit and sporting bright blue vinyl gloves and overshoes, emerged into the sunlight and spoke to Lyons who was standing just at the entrance to the temporary structure.

"I know, I know," the doctor said before Lyons could open her mouth, "when did she die and what killed her? Well, as for timing, I'd say she has been dead for twenty-four hours or more, but not much more. Rigor mortis is beginning to dissipate now. Probably sometime between seven and ten yesterday morning. As to the cause of death, I'd say the two enormous smacks to the back of the head with something very hard, wielded with considerable force, may have something to do with it. But that needs to be confirmed at the PM."

"Any identification, Doctor?" Fahy asked.

"That's for you lot to look after, Sergeant. I'm just a humble medic, after all."

Lyons thought to herself that the good doctor was in flying form this morning, but said nothing.

Fahy, who had stayed close to the gate talking to the uniformed officer, walked over in the direction of the tent where she noticed that yellow stepping plates had been put down to preserve any possible footprint evidence. From outside the makeshift structure, she called, "Sinéad, is it OK if I come in? It's Sally."

"Yes, of course, Sally, but mind where you walk."

Inside the tent, Loughran was bent down examining the corpse carefully. She had a magnifying glass in her hand and was focused on the back of the dead woman's head where two dark crimson patches were staining the victim's chestnut hair, some of which appeared to be missing entirely.

"Cripes! Someone didn't like her very much, did they?" Fahy said.

"Tell me about it. But I suppose you want to know who she is. Hang on a minute, I'm just finished here. We'll turn her over and see if there's anything in her pockets."

Sinéad Loughran beckoned to the white-suited photographer who was standing up taking photographs all around the body. The two of them gently gripped the dead woman's right side and turned her on her back. The cold, empty eyes of the young woman stared up at them from a pasty face with a bluish tone.

"Looks like she's taken a bit of a bruising to the face as well," Loughran said, "but that could have been from where she fell if it was on the road. Let's see what we can find to identify her."

Sinéad opened the coat that was still buttoned on the body of the young woman. Around her neck there was a black lanyard, and attached to it was a small plastic card with the name of the hotel and 'Aoife Gilpin' in bold black letters beneath it. Fahy relayed the information to Lyons who was still standing at the opening.

"Well, that's that then," Lyons said. "I'd better go and tell Séan. I suspect he'll want to go on up to the house and inform the parents. God, they'll be destroyed."

Fahy and Lyons joined Mulholland who was standing a little way off on the grass, looking grim. Fahy repeated the news about the dead woman's identity.

Séan Mulholland took the news of the young woman's death better than Lyons had hoped. He had a feeling that the body would be that of Aoife Gilpin, and he had prepared himself in any case.

"Are you OK to go up to the house and break the bad news, Séan?" Lyons said.

"Yes, of course. I'll get Mary to stay up there with them for the rest of the day anyway. She may be of some comfort to them, but it's a terrible thing. Tell me, Maureen, is there any sign of any, you know, interference?"

"By that I presume you mean was she sexually assaulted, Séan. No, there's no sign of anything like that. Her clothing appears to be intact. Her top coat was still buttoned up. But of course, we can't be sure till Dodd performs the PM."

Lyons could feel the man's natural empathy coming through in his words and his demeanour as he walked away slowly to deliver the awful news.

Lyons spoke to Fahy.

"Sally, can you get whoever is available and start asking around at the few houses hereabouts. Give it a few minutes till Séan has informed the Gilpins. We don't want the grapevine to get to them first. I'm going down to the hotel to ask questions. Follow me on down when you have things organised."

"OK, boss. Any initial thoughts?" Fahy said.

"Let's see how things work out during the day. And could you ask Pascal to set up a room at the station. See if he has a spare PC and a whiteboard. We'll convene there a bit later. Call me if anything develops."

Lyons set off on foot to walk back down Fuchsia Lane towards the hotel where Aoife had been employed. She had only gone a short distance when her phone started to ring.

"Maureen, it's Séan. Look, I forgot to tell you in all the fuss, but when I got to Fuchsia Lane initially, there were a number of plastic refuse sacks partly across the road and in the ditch. There were four of them in all. I put them in the boot of my car. I don't know if they are important, but I'll keep them safe in any case."

"Oh, right, Séan. Maybe you could give them to Sinéad to bring back into Galway. They may have some forensic value."

"Oh, right. Yes, I'll do that."

Lyons was a bit annoyed that Séan Mulholland had forgotten about what could be significant evidence, but she conceded that these were pretty extraordinary circumstances.

Chapter Four

Lyons had only gone another few paces when her phone rang again. She answered it promptly, thinking that it might be some important development in this peculiar case.

"Lyons," she said, not looking at the screen to see who the caller was.

"Maureen, it's Sheila, have you got a minute?"

"Oh, hi, Sheila, yes, sure, what's up?"

Sheila was Maureen Lyons' sister. She lived with her husband, Séamus, and two children on what had been the family farm out in Athenry. When Lyons' father had passed, the farm was left to the two of them, being the only offspring. Maureen and Shelia had come to an arrangement that Sheila and Séamus would run the place, but Maureen would retain an interest, and draw some income from it when times were good. It had worked well for all concerned.

"God, Maureen, I'm here in the hospital. Séamus is after taking a heart attack, I think. He was out working the lower ten-acre earlier, and I went to take him his elevenses, and there he was lying on the ground, barely conscious," Sheila said tearfully.

"Oh my God, that's terrible, Sheila. Is he OK?"

"I don't know, Maureen. I called an ambulance, and as luck would have it, there was one in the area. They got to the farm in under ten minutes. But as soon as we arrived here, they whisked him away, and I can't find out anything."

"OK, Sheila. I'm on my way. What ward is he in?"

"It's the cardiac ward, St Brigid's, on the second floor of the main building here at the Regional."

"Right. Go and get a hot sugary drink for yourself. I'll be there in half an hour or less."

"Thanks, Maureen. Are you sure it's OK?"

"Yes, of course. See you soon."

She found Sally Fahy and told her about the call she had received from her sister.

"I'm going to have to ask you to take over, Sally. Get Eamon Flynn to come out to you too, and maybe you'd explain to Séan why I've suddenly vanished. I was just on my way down to the hotel to ask some questions. Maybe Eamon or someone could do that."

"Right, boss. Don't worry. We'll manage. I hope your brother-in-law is OK. We'll all be thinking of him."

"Thanks, Sally. I'll call you when I know what's happening."

The next call Maureen Lyons made was to Superintendent Hays.

"Mick, it's me. Listen, I've had a call from Sheila. Séamus has been taken into the University Hospital with a heart attack. I'm on my way there now. I've left Sally in charge out in Roundstone, but you might want to give her a call. A local girl has been murdered by the look of things, and it needs a senior officer to oversee it."

"Oh, shit, Maureen love, I'm so sorry to hear that. Is Séamus OK?"

"I don't know. Sheila said they're working on him at the moment, but she's finding it hard to get any information."

University Hospital Galway is fortunately positioned on the west side of the city, so Lyons didn't have to do battle with the notorious Galway traffic on her way there. When she arrived, she parked in the large area to the left of the main entrance, and went in search of St Brigid's ward on the second floor as Sheila had directed.

"Hi, Sheila. How's he doing?"

"Hi, Maureen. They say he's stable for the moment, but quite weak. They've operated on him, and put two stents into his arteries. That's apparently what caused it. They say it's up to him now. He will either improve, or not, over the next twelve hours or so."

Lyons stood behind her sister and rested her hand on her shoulder.

"God, this is awful. It's good that you found him when you did. I suppose you could say he was lucky," Lyons said.

"That's what the doctor said. He said another half an hour lying out there in the cold, and it could have been very different," said Sheila, sobbing quietly.

"What about out beyond? Do you need any arrangements made for the farm, or the kids?"

"No, it's all fine. Mrs Whelan from down the road is going to see to the children, and Tommy and Séan-Óg will look after the farm."

"Oh, well that's something. It's great to have good neighbours. What about you? Do you need a coffee or something to eat?"

The nurse dabbed a sponge stick into a beaker of water that had been left on the locker and gently rubbed it against Séamus's lips.

"No, well, maybe a coffee. I didn't manage to get one earlier. Could you get one for me. I think there's a canteen of sorts downstairs."

"Sure, no problem. I'll go foraging. Back in a few minutes."

Lyons was shocked to see her brother-in-law quite so indisposed. But as soon as she got clear of the ward, she took out her mobile phone, checked for messages, and called Sally Fahy.

"Hi, Sally, it's me. What's the story?"

"Hi, boss. I'm still here on Fuchsia Lane. The doctor is just finishing up. They're going to take the body back into town shortly. I think Eamon is coming out to talk to the people in the hotel, and Séan has gone up to the house to see the parents," Fahy said.

"OK. Has Sinéad Loughran found anything of interest?"

"Yes. They found what they think may have been the weapon used. It's a short piece of scaffolding tube, and it has some very small traces of blood and hair at one end. Sinéad has bagged it up. It was in the ditch. Oh, and Superintendent Hays has been in touch to see if we need anything. But I told him we're OK for now."

"Is that it? Nothing else?" Lyons said.

"That's it. Are you at the hospital?" Fahy said.

"Yes, I'm here with Sheila and her husband."

"How is he?"

"So-so. We'll know more in a few hours apparently. Any idea when Dr Dodd is going to do the PM?"

"He said he'll try to get to it this afternoon. Maybe, as you're there, you could attend, or maybe that's not appropriate," Sally Fahy said.

"That's a good idea. Ask him to call me when he knows what's what. I'm not supposed to have my phone on in here, but I'll leave it on vibrate. And could you get Eamon to call me when he's got some news from the hotel."

"Yes, sure. I'll catch you later."

"Yes, thanks, bye."

Lyons went and procured two cups of what passed for coffee from the hospital canteen. When she got back to the ward, a doctor in a white coat with a stethoscope around his neck was talking to Sheila, and the nurse was still seated beside Séamus.

Sheila introduced Lyons who said, "How's he doing, Doc?"

"Pretty well. He's a bit woozy from the anaesthetic, but that's to be expected. But his vital signs are all good. There's some scarring to the heart, but it's not severe. I expect him to make a full recovery over time, but he'll have to take it very easy for a few weeks, and there will be some lifestyle changes coming too. But we can discuss that later," the doctor said in a rather matter-of-fact way.

"Nice to meet you, ladies. I'll be back later to see how he's doing," the doctor said, and with that he left quickly, no doubt on his way to another poorly patient.

"Well, that's very encouraging, Sheila. Looks as if he'll be as right as rain in no time," Lyons said.

"Yes. But I wonder what the doctor meant by lifestyle changes?" Sheila said.

"He'll be on medication for a while. Probably Plavix for a year or so, and of course statins as well, and maybe an anti-coagulant like Apixaban or Warfarin," the nurse said.

"Oh, right. What about exercise and activity?" Sheila said.

"Well, it's not really for me to say, but any form of strenuous lifting is probably out, and he shouldn't work with his arms above his head. There will be an exercise regime proposed for him too, but nothing too difficult. He looks like a fit man to me," the nurse said.

Following another twenty minutes of more or less silence, Lyons started to feel a bit restless, and her sister sensed it.

"You go on, Maureen. He's out of danger now, and I'll stay with him for the rest of the day," Sheila said.

"OK. I'm not much help here anyway. But I'll come back in later on and sit with him if you want to get off and see the children," Lyons said.

"Don't worry. They'll manage. There's plenty of food in the freezer."

"OK. Well, I'll see you later anyway."

Lyons leaned in and squeezed Séamus's hand, and then left the ward, trying to refocus on the case that was going on out in Roundstone with some difficulty.

Chapter Five

Sergeant Séan Mulholland took the four black plastic sacks out of the boot of his old Saab, and gave them to Sinéad Loughran, explaining where and how he had found them.

"Thanks, Sergeant. I'll take them back into town and see if they can tell us anything, but I'm not too hopeful."

Mulholland then got into his car, and manoeuvred it out of the tangle of vehicles deftly, till he could point it back along the N341 towards the Gilpins' house. He wasn't looking forward to what awaited him there. With nearly forty years' service in An Garda Síochána, he had only been involved in a small handful of murders, and he didn't like anything to do with them. "If this is what policing in these parts has come to, maybe it's time I gave it up," he said to himself as he approached "Seaview".

The front door of the house was open as Séan Mulholland approached. He pushed it fully open gently, and called out, not very loudly, "Hello, the house."

A moment later, a tall, trim man, with salt-and-pepper hair, neatly coiffed, wearing corduroy trousers and a check flannel shirt, open at the neck, appeared.

"Ah, Sergeant Mulholland, come in, come in. Any news?"

Mulholland removed his peaked cap, and advanced into the property. He gestured towards the door to the right of the hall with his hat, where voices were coming from.

"Oh, yes, sorry, we're in here."

The front room of the house, which validated the property's name, had a large picture window overlooking the shore. It was hard to believe that such tragedy could be perpetrated in this tranquil environment. Inside, Mrs Gilpin and Mary Fallon were seated on a sofa, and there was evidence that Mr Gilpin had been sitting in an armchair off to the side. Gilpin invited Séan Mulholland to sit, but he remained standing. All eyes turned to Mulholland whose grim expression foretold of bad news to come.

Mulholland acknowledged the occupants of the room.

"Mr and Mrs Gilpin, I'm very sorry to have to tell you that the body of a young woman has been found in a field just off Fuchsia Lane. Obviously, we need formal identification, but the woman had a hotel pass around her neck with your daughter's name on it. Aoife."

Total silence followed the announcement. Mrs Gilpin started to weep silently, and Mary Fallon moved closer to the woman, putting her arm around her shoulder in an attempt to console her.

Gerald Gilpin said, rather unnecessarily, "Are you sure it's her, Sergeant?"

Mulholland just nodded slightly. He didn't want to have to repeat himself. He cleared his throat. "She'll be taken back to the University Hospital in a while. Maybe, Mr Gilpin, you could come in tomorrow morning for us? I can send a car."

"Yes, of course. No, don't bother with the car, I'll drive myself. Can I get you a drink or something?"

"No thanks, you're grand, Mr Gilpin. Mary will stay here with you until later and get you anything you need. Is there anyone that we can get to come over?"

"Brigid's sister lives out the far side of Clifden. I'll give her a call in a while and ask her if she could come."

"Right. I'm very sorry, Mr Gilpin, Mrs Gilpin. I'd best be off now. There's a lot to do. Mary can contact me if there's anything. Could I just have a word outside, Mary, for a minute?"

"Yes, of course, Sergeant."

When they were outside, Mulholland said to the junior officer, "That was a bit of a funny reaction from Mr Gilpin, don't you think?"

"I didn't notice, Sergeant, to be honest," Fallon said.

"Well, never mind. Are you OK with this, Mary?"

"Yes, fine, Sergeant. I'm not totally sure how to handle everything, but I'll be OK. It's just a matter of keeping them company and acting as liaison I suppose, at least till Mrs Gilpin's sister gets here."

"There's a bit more to it than that, Mary. When the dreadful news has sunk in a bit, see if you can find out something about Aoife. They'll be keen to talk about her in a wee while. Try and find out as much as you can about her; what she did with her time off – that sort of thing. And see if she had a laptop computer, or a mobile phone. We didn't find one about her person. If you get a chance, give me a call a bit later on."

"Yes, OK, Sergeant. Have you any idea what happened to Aoife?"

"Apart from the fact that she was killed, you mean. No. Did you know her at all?"

"I'd seen her at the hotel a few times, that's all. Sometimes I'd go around there at lunchtime for a quick sandwich with Pascal. She seemed very nice. A bit quiet, but pleasant enough."

"OK. Well, you'd better get back in there. Stay focused, Mary, and we'll talk later."

* * *

Maureen Lyons left her sister at the bedside of her husband. She made Sheila promise to call her if there was any change in Séamus's condition, and said she would be in touch later on in any case.

Once outside, she called Sally Fahy.

"Hi, Sally. Can I have an update?"

"Hello, boss. I'm still at the site. Sinéad and her people are examining everything carefully. The body has been taken away now, and Dr Dodd is gone."

"Right. Has Séan come back from the Gilpins' house yet?"

"No, not yet. And I had a call from Eamon. He's down at the hotel asking questions. We've arranged to meet in Roundstone station when we're all done. How are things there?"

"Ah, you know. Not too bad. Séamus had a heart attack, but the ambulance got to him fairly quickly. He's had an operation here in Galway. I think he'll be OK, but Sheila got a terrible fright."

"God, that's awful. I hope he'll be OK. What are you going to do, boss?"

"What, now? I think I'll hang around here at the hospital and hook up with Dr Dodd when he gets here. He might do the post-mortem pretty quickly if I'm hovering around and then we might get some insight into this dreadful business. Is Mary OK?" Lyons said.

"Yes, I think so. She's up at the house with the Gilpins."

"Right. Why don't we agree to get together in Roundstone at around six. I should be finished here by then. Get Eamon, Mary, Pascal, Sergeant Mulholland, and anyone else you can think of together, and if there's any change in plan, I'll let you know."

"OK. Will do. Thanks."

Lyons walked around to the back of the main hospital building where the entrance to the morgue was located. As she approached, Dr Dodd's shiny black Lexus rolled into the car park, followed by an anonymous-looking black Mercedes van.

"Hello, Inspector. What are you doing here?" Dodd asked rather abruptly when he was standing next to his car in the car park.

"Nice to see you too, Doctor. Never mind what I'm doing here. Do you think you might get around to the post-mortem on the Gilpin woman this afternoon?" Lyons said.

"Well, as it's for you, I suppose so. Let me get inside and see what else awaits, and then I'll know better. Come with me if you like."

The two fell in step and made their way to Dodd's office which was small, but neatly ordered, and contained a desk, a side table, a few chairs, and several filing cabinets. But the room was clean, and very tidy, with just a few manilla folders stacked at the edge of the workspace. A computer screen, keyboard, mouse, and office telephone occupied the remainder of the desk space.

Dodd washed his hands in the small sink provided in a corner of the room and sat down at his desk. He nudged the mouse, and his computer screen came to life. After a moment scrolling down through a few emails he looked up and said, "All right. It looks as if I'm clear for the afternoon. Why don't we make a start?"

Lyons didn't like post-mortems. She was all right with the preliminaries – the close examination of the whole body; the removal of items snagged in the dead person's hair or clothing; the investigation of any surface wounds; but when it came to opening the cadaver, as it invariably did, by the use of a scalpel or other gruesome tool, Lyons struggled. Here was a woman, after all, who up to a couple of days ago had been going about her everyday life, whatever that entailed. And now she was reduced to a specimen for a pathologist on a cold slab of stainless steel waiting to be sliced open.

Aoife Gilpin's clothes had been removed, and she was covered in just a narrow strip of cream-coloured muslin across her genitalia to preserve some modicum of dignity. Dr Julian Dodd circled the body, leaning in closely at various stages to examine the woman's skin, before stopping at the head to examine her wounds more thoroughly.

"Inspector, do you know if this woman was married?" Dodd asked.

Lyons was somewhat taken aback by the question.

"No, I don't think so, but I'm not a hundred per cent certain. Why do you ask?"

"Well, unless I'm very much mistaken, and I rarely am, your Miss Gilpin here is, or should I say, was, with child."

Lyons' eyes immediately focused on the bare belly of the corpse, but could see no obvious bulge, although with Aoife Gilpin lying on her back, it could have been hard to detect in any case.

"Are you sure, Doc? How can you tell?" Lyons said.

"When you've been at this game as long as I have, Inspector, you just know. First trimester, I'd wager. Maybe eight or nine weeks. But I'll know for certain when we open her up. And before you ask, the foetus will not have survived beyond a few hours, if that."

"Bloody hell! That's all we need," Lyons said in exasperation.

Chapter Six

The Bertraghboy Bay Hotel was relatively quiet when Inspector Eamon Flynn entered the lobby mid-morning, having driven out from Galway. He introduced himself to the girl at the small and rather crowded front desk, which was overflowing with brochures of various activities that residents could partake of in the area.

"Good morning, Stella," he said, squinting at the small gold badge pinned to the receptionist's jacket bearing her name. "My name is Detective Inspector Flynn. I wonder if I could have a word with the manager? What's his name, by the way?"

"Good morning, sir," Stella said with a slight accent placing her somewhere from Eastern Europe, Flynn surmised.

"That would be Mrs McMadden. Hold on a minute and I'll see if I can find her for you."

Stella slipped out from behind the desk and went off down the narrow corridor towards the back of the premises leaving Flynn to observe the place. The building he was standing in was certainly old. It probably dated from the mid to late nineteenth century, but it had been extended more than once by the look of things. The latest extension was a rather soulless strip of concrete rooms stretching back from the side of the original building, and by counting the windows, Flynn calculated that it housed ten of the fifteen rooms the hotel provided for guests. The remainder of the accommodation would be upstairs in the original building, and although they would perhaps have more character to them, they could be draughty and possible noisy, he mused.

Interrupting his imaginings, Eileen McMadden arrived with Stella bringing up the rear from somewhere deep inside the building.

"Good morning, officer. How can I help you today?" Mrs McMadden said, holding out her hand to be shaken.

"Is there somewhere we could talk, Mrs McMadden?"

The woman looked at him a little quizzically, and it seemed to take her a moment to process the request, but then she said, "Yes, of course, here in the lounge." She indicated a large room laid out with round tables and chairs just off the reception area.

Inside the lounge, a small bar was set up against the back wall, with three beer taps and an array of bottles, some of which hung suspended with optics beneath them, and a few dozen glasses of various sizes. The furniture in the room was worn, but still serviceable, and the navy carpet with a small pink floral medallion arranged in a geometric shape all over, was, Flynn thought, probably the newest addition to the room. Plain velvet curtains that looked rather tired adorned the double aspect windows, and a series of two-headed wall lights provided the illumination. The smell of stale beer just about managed to overwhelm the scent of furniture polish that had been liberally applied recently to each of the tables.

Mrs McMadden indicated a spot near the window that looked out to the side of the building, and the pair sat down.

"May I offer you some refreshment, Inspector? Tea, coffee, or perhaps something a little stronger," the woman said with a rather cheesy smile.

"Eh, no thanks, Mrs McMadden, I'm fine for now. May I ask if you have a woman by the name of Aoife Gilpin working for you here?"

"Yes. Yes, we do. But I'm afraid she hasn't turned up for the last two days. It's most unlike her. Why do you ask?"

Flynn noticed that the hotel proprietor looked quite uneasy talking about the dead woman. She shifted restlessly in her chair, and avoided eye contact with Flynn.

"You must have heard about her, Mrs McMadden. What have you been told?"

"It's probably just gossip. You know what this place is like. The locals have little to amuse themselves, so you hear all sorts. Why? What has happened?"

"I'm sorry to have to tell you, Mrs McMadden, Aoife Gilpin was found dead not three hundred metres from here early this morning. She had been killed, I'm afraid. We're treating it as murder," Flynn said.

"Dear God, that's dreadful. The poor girl. And her parents! Oh, this is just too awful," Mrs McMadden said as tears began to flow.

Flynn waited for the initial shock to pass. He had, unfortunately, seen this reaction all too often when he had to impart bad news to those close to murder victims.

"Can you tell me a little about Aoife, Mrs McMadden? How long had she been working here?"

"Let me see, it would be about two and a half years now. Yes, she started in April that year and she's been with us ever since. She was usually very reliable. A quiet girl, but a good worker. She never gave us any trouble. But what happened to her? Was she run over or something, or knocked off her bicycle?" Mrs McMadden said.

"Did she have any particular friends here at the hotel, Mrs McMadden?" Flynn said, dodging the question.

"We're all pretty friendly, Inspector. It's a small staff, so we know each other quite well. Aoife is well liked and as far as I can see, got on with everyone." Mrs McMadden paused her short speech which Eamon Flynn felt sounded a little too well rehearsed. "Oh, look, this is too awful," she went on. "Do you mind if I get myself a drink? Can I get you anything?"

"No thanks, but by all means get something for yourself," Flynn said.

Mrs McMadden got up and went behind the bar. She took a glass and poured herself a good measure of brandy from a half-full bottle and returned to the table. She took a decent swig of the liquor and put the glass down.

"I don't usually drink brandy, but needs must," she said.

"Do you know if Aoife had a boyfriend at all, Mrs McMadden?"

"I couldn't say, Inspector. I'm not privy to the staff's personal lives outside the hotel, but you could ask Stella. She might know. Do you think we should close the place for a day or two?"

"That's up to you. We will need to talk to some of the other staff members, but I'm sure the Gilpins would appreciate the gesture."

"Very well. If you have nothing further to ask me then, I'll go and make the arrangements."

Mrs McMadden stood up, downed the remainder of her drink in one go, and was setting off when Flynn called to her.

"Could you ask Stella to pop in for a moment. I won't keep her long. Thanks."

Flynn was a little surprised that the news of Aoife Gilpin's death hadn't reached Mrs McMadden and the rest of the people in the hotel before he arrived. Roundstone was a very small place with a highly active grapevine, and the establishment was a hub of a kind, so the fact that Mrs McMadden hadn't heard about it was puzzling.

Stella, who was in her early twenties and no more than five foot tall, with a pretty face and dark blonde shoulder-length hair, came into the room soon after the proprietor had left. She was wearing a navy skirt, matching jacket, and pale-yellow blouse which Flynn assumed was a uniform of sorts for her work as a receptionist.

"Come in, Stella. Sit down for a moment. I won't keep you long."

It was clear from Stella's demeanour that she had been told of her colleague's death. She was crying and held a few tissues in her hand which she used to dab her bright blue eyes every few moments. She took a seat in the same chair that Mrs McMadden had occupied a few minutes earlier.

"You've obviously heard about Aoife, Stella. I'm very sorry to bring such bad news. When did you find out?" Flynn said.

"We heard something last night, but it was just a rumour. None of us wanted to believe it, but Mrs McMadden says that Aoife has been killed, is that right?"

"I'm afraid that is correct, Stella. Yes. She was found earlier this morning. Can I ask what rumour you heard and from whom?"

"It was just last night in the bar. There was some talk amongst the locals that Aoife had gone missing, but that's all. But no one said she had been killed," Stella said.

She started to weep silently again, and Flynn gave her a minute to steady herself.

"Did you know Aoife well, Stella?"

"I guess so. There's only four of us that work here regularly apart from the kitchen staff, so we were quite good friends."

"Did you ever socialise with Aoife, like go out at night with her, or go to parties or anything?" Flynn said.

"No. We don't really have much time for that, and there's nowhere to go around here anyway. But sometimes we'd go for a drink in one of the other hotels just for a change of scene."

"Did Aoife have a boyfriend at all, Stella?"

"I don't think so, no. But she may have done. She was quite a private person like that."

"But you never saw her in the company of a lad here, or at one of the other bars at all?"

"No. I didn't."

"Do you know what she did on her days off?"

"She used to like to go into Galway for shopping. She had a few friends in the city too, and she told me she'd meet them occasionally, but she never told me any of the details."

"Do you have a boyfriend, Stella?"

The girl flushed a little before answering.

"Yes. I go out with one of the boys from the kitchen. He's a chef. There are two. Conor is the junior chef, and there's an older man, Fergal, who runs the kitchen."

"And what are the McMaddens like to work for? You can be honest with me, Stella, it won't go any further."

"Fair, I suppose. Mrs McMadden can be a bit bossy at times, but she's not bad, and we are treated fairly well."

"What about Mr McMadden?"

"We don't see him too often. He has another business, I think. But he's here at weekends and sometimes during the week too. He's nicer to us. He often gives us a generous tip if the bar is busy, especially the girls."

Flynn made a careful mental note of that little nugget of information, but decided not to pursue it further, for the moment at least.

Chapter Seven

The team reassembled in the Garda station in Roundstone late that first afternoon. Lyons had called her sister again before leaving the city, but Sheila had reassured her that she had everything under control.

"They're keeping him in overnight just for observation, but they said that the danger is passed now, and he should be OK to go home tomorrow, provided he follows the rules that they are giving him," Sheila had told her sister.

"Are you sure there's nothing you want me to do, Sheila?" Lyons said.

"No, it's fine. I'll get off shortly now too and come back in the morning. The kids will need their dinner, and I want to check that the farm is OK. And Séamus is in good hands here."

"OK, then, but if anything changes, I want to know about it. Promise you'll call."

"Yes, of course."

* * *

Lyons had spent the journey back out to Roundstone mulling over Sheila's new situation. Things had changed with his heart attack, and she hoped that both Séamus and her sister would recognise that and act accordingly.

As she turned off the N59 onto the R341 to take her to the village, she tried to focus her thoughts on the matter in hand, but it wasn't easy. When she had parked her car and gone inside, she quickly managed to address the current crime under investigation and once she had been armed with a cup of tea, she brought the little group together.

Sally Fahy was the first to speak.

"How's your brother-in-law, boss?"

"I think he's OK, thanks, Sally. He's had an angioplasty at the hospital, and it all went pretty well, so I think he'll be fine in a few days."

"Good, that's a relief, then," Fahy said.

"Yes, but for now, I need to focus on what's been going on here. Can we go around the group to bring me up to date please?"

Each of the team told their story in turn, so that after fifteen minutes, Lyons was completely up to speed.

"Well, I suppose you've heard that Aoife Gilpin was pregnant. So straight away, there's more to this thing than we first thought. Has Sinéad Loughran been in touch with any results from the weapon or the plastic bags that Sergeant Mulholland lifted from the road?"

"The length of scaffolding tubing was clean, boss, apart from the blood and hair stuck to the end of it, which, as suspected, turned out to belong to the victim. Sinéad hasn't finished with the plastic bags yet. They were stuffed with cardboard and polystyrene waste it seems. She'll have more on them a bit later."

"What about the parents, Mary? Did you find out anything useful up at the family home?"

"Not really, Inspector. The parents aren't aware of any boyfriend that their daughter had. They said she was very busy at the hotel, and never talked about a partner, nor did she ever bring anyone home. They let me look in her room, and I took away a laptop. I have it here," the young officer said. She lifted up an evidence bag containing the item and showed it to the rest of the team.

"OK. Well, someone made her pregnant. That's what we need to focus on for now. We need to know who the father of her baby is and talk to him as a matter of urgency. Eamon, did you find out anything useful in that regard at the hotel?"

"No, sorry, boss. I spoke to the owner, a Mrs McMadden, and to another one of the staff, Stella, the receptionist. Neither of them said anything about a boyfriend. All they said was that Aoife liked to go into Galway at the weekends if she had time off for shopping," Flynn said.

"Hmm... OK. We need to follow that up. Tomorrow, Mary, can you go back out to the Gilpins and see if Aoife ever stayed overnight in Galway, and if so, where she stayed and who with. Or at least who did she say she stayed with. Do you think the folks at the hotel were being straight with you, Eamon?"

"I'm not sure, to be honest. Mrs McMadden struck me as a rather cold woman, and the receptionist lassie was a bit coy too when I asked her about boyfriends. She might be worth another chat. Oh, by the way, they've closed the place for a few days out of respect for the victim and the family."

"Right then. Plans for tomorrow. I'll be back out here before ten to get things organised. I want you, Pascal, to do a really good probe around the town. Find out everything you can about Aoife Gilpin, and don't be too gentle. We need to establish a motive for this killing as quickly as we can. Get Mary to help you. Turn over every stone in the village. Speak to everyone who lives here. Find out who was staying at all the hotels and B&Bs as well, and see if any of them have form for anything. Let's see if we can establish a person or persons of interest by close of play tomorrow. Eamon, will you follow up with Sinéad? There must be some bits of evidence either on Aoife's person or in the vicinity of the crime. I doubt if this is the perfect murder we hear so much about but rarely encounter. Sally, I want you back in Galway doing background checks on the Gilpins and the McMaddens. Get as much information as you can about everyone connected to the dead woman. And see if you can get into Aoife's bank account too. See if there's anything unusual there. I'll take her computer back to John O'Connor and see what he can get out of it. OK, everyone?"

A murmur of assent went around the room.

* * *

Almost as soon as Lyons was back on the road, her thoughts turned once again to her sister and her dilemma. She couldn't help but play "what if" in her head as far as their family was concerned. She knew her brother-in-law would have to change his lifestyle, or risk another, perhaps more serious, cardiac event, but knowing the man, she felt that it would not be easy for him. And, as usual, her sister would probably have to take the brunt of her husband's frustration. Things were not going to be easy for them, and as she passed Maam Cross, she tried to figure out how she could provide support without seeming to interfere.

Lyons' thoughts were interrupted by the phone in her car springing to life. It was her partner, Mick Hays, calling.

"Hi, Mick," Lyons said as she answered the phone using the hands-free device.

"Hi. Where are you?" he said.

"Let's see, just between Maam Cross and Oughterard. I'll be back home in about an hour. What about you?"

"I'm still at Mill Street, but I'll be finished soon. Any news of Séamus?"

"Yes, he's fine, or so Sheila is saying. They're hoping he'll be sent home tomorrow, but I don't know, it all seems a bit quick to me."

"I'm sure they know what they are doing. They wouldn't release him unless he was OK. Anyway, how are you for food?"

"God, I haven't thought about it. Now that you mention it, I'm pretty hungry. I didn't manage to get any lunch. Things are a bit crazy out in Roundstone."

"OK. Well, why don't we meet in town and we can go and get something then. I'll fix up a booking somewhere. Give me a call when you're past Moycullen."

"OK, thanks, I'll do that. See ya," Lyons said.

For the rest of the drive Lyons reflected on how lucky she had been to find Mick Hays. Relationships between member of the force were generally frowned upon by management, but somehow, this one seemed to have worked well for all concerned. They had been together for quite a while now, and even Superintendent Finbarr Plunkett had to admit that there seemed to be no downside to the arrangement. Once she was free of the minor bottleneck that always seemed to occur as you drove through Moycullen, she called Mick Hays again.

"Hi. It's me. So where are you going to take me for a slap-up dinner then?" she said.

"Ah, what would you say to Kirwan's. My treat," Hays said.

"Excellent, sir. See you there in about fifteen minutes."

"Great."

Chapter Eight

Lyons was up and about very early the following day. Hays and herself had enjoyed a delicious meal at Kirwan's the previous evening. Mick Hays had the good sense to keep the conversation light. He managed to avoid mentioning the murdered girl out at Roundstone entirely, and any lull in the conversation was filled with enquiries about Maureen Lyons' brother-in-law. Hays was sensitive to the fact that Lyons was the SIO on the case, and while he would provide any help and support that was required if it were asked for, he didn't want her to think that he was muscling in on her patch.

So, when Lyons arrived in Mill Street the following morning at just after eight o'clock, she was feeling revived and well able for whatever the day would bring. Garda John O'Connor, who had great skill with anything to do with computers or mobile phones, was preparing to probe Aoife Gilpin's laptop that Lyons had brought in for him.

"See if you can get into that one, John, and if you do, I want to know what sites she was looking up recently, and of course any relevant emails too," Lyons said.

"Right, boss. Did she have a mobile phone at all?"

"I'm sure she had, but we haven't found it. Not yet, in any case. I'll let you know if it turns up. I have a photograph of the woman here too that Mary Fallon was given out at her parents' house. Can you make me a few good clean copies of it and hand them around – see if anyone recognises her? I know it's a long shot, but you never know."

"Sure, no problem," O'Connor said obligingly.

Lyons went into her office. She would leave again in a short while for Roundstone where she had asked the team to gather for ten o'clock. There was a lot to do. She spent half an hour catching up with emails and various bulletins that had appeared in her inbox, and then she wondered if she should call her sister. She decided, given the early hour, that she would leave it for a while as Sheila would no doubt be busy getting the kids out to school. She was just about to leave when one of the female Gardaí that Lyons recognised from the roads policing unit knocked on her door.

"Excuse me, Inspector, may I have a word?" the woman said.

"Yes, of course. Come in. What's up?"

"Well, it's just this photograph that John O'Connor was handing around. I think I've seen the woman recently."

"Oh? That's interesting. Have a seat and tell me about it," Lyons said.

The Garda sat down in front of Lyons' desk.

"We were out doing a checkpoint for tax and insurance just near the big shopping centre last Saturday night. We stopped a BMW being driven by a guy who had a female passenger, and I'm nearly certain it was the girl in the photograph. We asked the driver for his licence, and he said it was in his briefcase in the boot of the car. He got out, and Peter, the other officer I was with, went to the back of the car and sure enough, his licence was produced."

"You don't remember the name of the driver, I suppose?"

"Well, that's the funny thing. The licence was in the name of Anthony Miller. But by this time the woman had also got out of the car to see what was going on, and she called to the driver and said something like, 'Is everything OK, Michael?' That's when I got a fairly good look at her, and I'm nearly certain it was the woman in your photograph."

"Did you get the registration number of the car?" Lyons asked.

"Yes. Peter did a check on the system to see that the car was insured, so it should be recorded. But the licence, tax and insurance were all in order, so we didn't detain them or anything. It's just that it took a bit longer than usual because of the fact that the licence was in the boot."

"Did you mention the discrepancy in the name to your colleague?"

"Yes, I did, but he said I must have heard incorrectly, but I'm sure I didn't," the young Garda said.

"OK. Well, thanks for that information. It could be very important. You didn't happen to find out where they were coming from or going to, did you?"

"No. Once everything checked out, they were keen to get going, so we just let them off."

"Right. Well could I ask you to get the number of the BMW for me. Here's my mobile number. Maybe you could text it through to me?" Lyons said, scribbling her number on a small yellow Post-it note and handing it to the Garda.

"Yes, of course. What happened to her – the woman in the photograph, I mean?"

"I'm afraid she was murdered. Her body was discovered in a field beside the road in Roundstone. Nasty business."

"Gosh. That's awful. I'd better go and follow this up for you, Inspector."

"Yes, thanks. And thanks for the information too. I've a feeling that will be very useful."

* * *

As Lyons was preparing to leave the station, she spotted Inspector Eamon Flynn arriving.

"Hi, Eamon. I'm just off back to Roundstone to continue with our investigations. I need you to see if you can track down an Anthony Miller who drives a dark-coloured BMW, but he may also go by the name of Michael," Lyons said.

"How do you mean?" Flynn said, obviously puzzled.

"I'm not sure. Just see if you can get an address. I'll have the reg number of the car a bit later and I'll send it through to you, that should help."

"OK. Whatever. Do you need any help out beyond?" Flynn said.

"No, I don't think so. I'm meeting Sally out there, and we have Pascal and Mary too, and some of Séan's men if we need them. I'll let you know if I do need extra help, though. Catch you later."

* * *

As Maureen Lyons drove out along the N59, her thoughts once again turned to her sister and her situation. She looked at the car's clock, and as it was showing 9:25, she decided it was a good time to call Sheila. She dialled the number, and the phone at the other end was answered on the second ring.

"Hi, Sheila. How's things? Did you get some sleep?"

"Oh, hi, Maureen. Well, sort of. The hospital was on. They're letting Séamus out after the doctor has done his rounds at eleven, so I'm heading over soon. I want to be there to hear what the doctor has to say."

"Yes, of course. Listen, sis, and I really mean this, if there's anything at all either Mick or myself can do, please let us know. We're keen to help out if at all possible."

"Thanks, Maureen, we will. I'm just trying to imagine Mick dressed in his full uniform milking a few cows!"

The two of them laughed.

"No, but seriously, don't be afraid to ask. How are the kids bearing up?" Lyons said.

"Ah, they're grand. Not a bother. I don't think they realise how serious it could have been, and I'm going to keep it that way."

"Good idea. Well, I'd better not delay you. I'll give you a call later, and be sure to give Séamus our best wishes."

"Of course. Thanks, Maureen."

Lyons was just navigating a bit of traffic that had built up in the centre of Oughterard, when her phone rang.

"Lyons," she said, not immediately recognising the number.

"Good morning, Inspector. It's Dr Dodd here. I just thought I'd give you a call. We found something on the dead woman from Roundstone."

"Oh, really. What's that then, Doc?" Lyons said. Once again, she sensed that the good doctor was building up to some great reveal which he was inclined to do. It sometimes drove Lyons mad.

"Yes. After we removed her clothing, tucked inside her jeans on the inside was a small pocket, and you'll never guess what we found in it."

"No, you're quite right, Doctor, I'll never guess, so maybe you could just tell me?" Lyons said, losing patience.

"She had a little mobile phone. You know, one of those small Nokia ones like we all used to have with buttons instead of a screen. Quite honestly, I think I prefer them to the latest ones. They're much simpler to use, and the battery lasts for such a long time."

"Yes, quite. Well, when Sinéad has dusted it for prints, maybe you could get it over to John O'Connor for us?" Lyons said.

"Or maybe he could come and get it? Sinéad has gone galivanting off in her big jeep back to Roundstone. She wants to do another sweep of the murder scene in case they've missed anything. But sometimes I think she just likes driving that thing."

Lyons capitulated. It was easier to ask O'Connor to do the necessary than argue all day with Dodd in any case. When she had finished the call with the pathologist, she called O'Connor and set him in motion.

Chapter Nine

When Lyons arrived at the small, whitewashed Garda station in Roundstone, there were already several cars parked alongside. Loughran's 4x4 was there, a Ford that she recognised as Jim Dolan's, a Garda from Clifden, as well as Mary Fallon's VW Golf.

When she got inside, her colleagues were all seated around a table drinking tea or coffee, and chatting about recent events.

Lyons joined them and gave them the information that they had received from the traffic cops about the BMW.

"Traffic sent me the reg number of the BMW and I've sent it on to Eamon. Let's see if we can find out anything about this Anthony, or Tony Miller, although he may actually be Michael something-or-other, so keep an open mind," she said. "Sinéad, have you got anywhere with the bags that Séan Mulholland lifted from the roadside out where Aoife was killed?"

"We're still working on them, boss. There was quite a bit of white polystyrene in two of them. We're trying to trace where that came from or what it was protecting before it was dumped, but it's not easy."

"That stuff is usually used for packing electronic stuff like TVs or fridges and the like," Mary Fallon said.

"Yes, but without the outer packaging to go with it, it's very difficult to trace. I have one of the team working on it though. He likes jigsaw puzzles," Loughran said. "And, boss, I was thinking," Loughran went on, "whoever attacked Aoife must have had a vehicle of some kind to make their getaway. And if they'd blocked the road with the bags, then that vehicle must have been parked for a while at least on the town side of the lane where she was killed, or nearby. I'm going to go back and have a good look in the dirt at the side of the lane and see if I can get anything. There's very little traffic on that road, so there may be something of value."

"Good idea, Sinéad. Has anyone told the Gilpins that their daughter was with child?" Lyons said.

The rest of the group looked from one to the other a little sheepishly.

"That will be a 'no' then," Lyons said. "Well, we'd better let them know and see what reaction that brings. Mary, you've been up at the house quite a bit. Let's you and I go up there when we've finished here and break the good news."

Mary Fallon said nothing, but she didn't look too pleased with the plan.

"Oh and, Pascal, while you are stirring things up locally, follow up on the car here in the village, and see if the driver is known. If he was out this way with Aoife, he might have bought fuel down at the pumps outside the shop. I know it's a bit of a long shot, but we have to try. Before we go, Mary, I want to call Eamon back in Galway to see if there's any news on the car. And, Jim, can you do some poking around about the Gilpin family. Find out what the father does for a living and anything else relevant. Give me a few minutes, Mary, and I'll be with you."

Lyons got up and went outside. Standing outside the building, Lyons couldn't help but admire her surroundings.

The sky was largely clear, with just a few cotton wool clouds moving lazily from east to west, and although it was cool, the autumnal light was flattering the place. She wondered to herself how such evil could prevail in such an idyllic location.

* * *

"Hi, Eamon, it's me."

"Morning, boss. What's up?"

"I'm out here in Roundstone. I was wondering if there's any news on the BMW or the driver? I think we need to track him down as a matter of urgency."

"Hang on a sec. Let's see. Oh, yes, I knew I'd seen something come in. You're not going to like this. Sorry, boss."

"Go on."

"We tracked down the owner's name and address for the BMW through the vehicle registration people. The car is registered to a Tony Miller, but I asked one of the uniformed guys to call around to the house, and guess what – it's a false address. Doesn't exist."

"Shit. Any other leads on this bloke? Like where the car was bought, or whatever?" Lyons said.

"I'm following up a few possibilities, but to be truthful, it's not looking too clever," Flynn said.

"OK. Look, Eamon, this whole thing is turning into a right old mystery. I think it's time we dug a little deeper on Aoife Gilpin. Could you see if Sally has got anywhere with her bank, and if so, get her account records. I know it's a long shot, but we need some kind of breakthrough here. And let's put out a bulletin for Tony Miller as a person of interest too. Circulate it nationally with the car registration details. Give me a call if you get anything."

"OK, will do."

* * *

When Lyons and Fallon arrived at the Gilpins' house, there was just one vehicle in the driveway. It was a large black Toyota Land Cruiser with a recent plate, but it was quite muddy. Walking past it to get to the front door, Lyons noticed that the front seats had quite a lot of waste cups and papers scattered around.

Both of Aoife's parents were at home, and although they both looked tired and drawn, Mrs Gilpin was still hospitable, offering tea or coffee to the officers.

Maureen Lyons and Mary Fallon carried out a well-practised routine. Lyons would sit the couple down and impart the bad news about their daughter while Mary Fallon would stay standing at the kitchen window and observe both parents carefully and form an impression of their reaction for later discussion.

When Lyons had their attention, she broke the news.

"As you know, we have now carried out a post-mortem on Aoife. The cause of her death is clear, but there's something else that may come as a bit of a surprise to you both," she said.

The two Gilpins stared at Lyons expectantly.

"Did either of you know that Aoife was expecting a baby?"

The colour drained from Mrs Gilpin's face and she started to sob loudly, clutching a bunch of paper tissues that Lyons felt had been her constant companion since the news of her daughter's death broke. Mr Gilpin reacted very differently.

"That's ridiculous! How dare you come here and try to besmirch Aoife's reputation like that. Aoife was a good girl. She didn't even have a boyfriend, for God's sake. You've got that wrong, Inspector, and if that's all you've come to say, I'd like you to leave right now," the man said, extending his hand to cover his wife's hand by way of consolation.

Lyons stayed put, and waited for the storm to pass. After a short interval when she sensed the moment was right, she spoke up again.

"Mr Gilpin, I can assure you that the pathologist, Dr Julian Dodd, would not be mistaken. I assume from what you have said that neither of you were aware of this?"

"Of course not. I still don't believe it. Who is this Dodd fella anyway? I'd like to speak to him."

"That's a little irregular, Mr Gilpin, but I'll see if I can get him to call you. He may be prepared to under the circumstances. I know this is very difficult for both of you," Lyons said, attempting to include Aoife's mother in the conversation without much success.

She looked directly at Mrs Gilpin.

"Are you sure Aoife wasn't seeing someone, Mrs Gilpin? Maybe she had a friend down at the hotel, or something. Or what about the times she went to Galway. Did she often stay over?"

Brigid Gilpin still said nothing, but her husband was happy to respond.

"She hasn't, hadn't, got a boyfriend, I told you. And when she stayed over in Galway sometimes it was with her girlfriends. The bus service out here at the weekends isn't up to much, so it was easier for her to say over sometimes and get the bus back out Sunday evening."

"And who were these friends that Aoife stayed with, Mr Gilpin?"

"I don't know. She was a grown woman, for God's sake. We didn't pry into her business."

Brigid Gilpin suddenly found her voice.

"Aoife mentioned a girl called Liz, or Lizzy. It might have been Faherty or O'Flaherty or something. I didn't pay much heed to it, to be honest."

"Do you know where this Liz girl lived, Mrs Gilpin?" Lyons asked.

"No. No, she didn't say. But it will be somewhere in the city."

"Do you know how Aoife came to know Liz at all?"

"No. She might have met her at the hotel or something, I'm not sure."

"OK, thanks. We'll follow that up with them. By the way, did Aoife have a mobile phone?" Mary Fallon asked.

"What sort of a question is that?" Gerald Gilpin said. "Of course she had. We bought her one of those new iPhone things for her Christmas, and she never let it out of her hand. Haven't you found it?"

"No, we haven't. Maybe you could give me the number for it and I'll see if we can track it down that way."

Brigid Gilpin scribbled a mobile number in pencil on a small piece of paper and handed it to Lyons without saying anything.

Lyons felt that the conversation with the bereaved parents had run its course, so she stood up, thanked them for their time, and nodded to Mary Fallon that it was time to go.

"I'll see if Dr Dodd would be prepared to give you a call later on, Mr Gilpin. I know he's quite busy, but I'm sure he will make the time as it's important to you."

On the way out of the house, Maureen Lyons happened to glance into the sitting room which was positioned at the front of the dwelling with the fabulous view that had given the property its name. She spotted a very large, and very new, flat screen television perched on a low oak table beside the fireplace.

Once they were safely back in the privacy of their car, Lyons said to Mary Fallon, "What did you make of that then?"

"Hard to say. I can't make up my mind if the father's reaction was perfectly normal, or if he protested a little too much," Fallon said.

"Yes, I know what you mean. He could just have thought that his Aoife was still an innocent little virgin, or there could be a bit more to it. What about the mother?" Lyons said.

"She's very hard to read, but I think she may have known more than she was letting on, don't you?" Mary Fallon said.

"I agree. God, why are families so bloody difficult! Anyway, we'd better see if we can track this Liz woman down. Can you get onto the hotel and see if they ever had a Liz Faherty or Liz O'Flaherty working there? I'll get Eamon to start poking around in Galway too, but it's a popular name, so it won't be easy. That is, if the woman exists at all!"

Chapter Ten

On the way back to Galway in the afternoon, Lyons called John O'Connor and asked him to start looking into Aoife Gilpin's iPhone.

"Get onto the airtime provider and see when it was last used either for inbound or outbound calls, and get them to send you three months of call records too. Then we can look for any frequently called numbers, although since she had the other phone tucked inside her jeans, it may not yield much."

"Right, boss. Are you coming back later?" O'Connor said.

"Yes, I'll be there in about an hour or a bit less depending on the traffic. Why? Anything specific?"

"It's just we should have something back from her bank by then. Her account was at the post office. The postmaster was a bit unhelpful at first, but I talked him around eventually," O'Connor said.

"Good, well done. Anything on her laptop?"

"I haven't had a chance to look at it yet, but I'll get to it later today."

"OK. Thanks, John. See you in a while."

Lyons continued her journey eastwards towards the city. When she was just passing Rosscahill, her phone rang. It was Mick Hays.

"Hi, Mick. Good to hear from you. What's the story?" Lyons said.

"Hi. Where are you?"

"I'm just on my way back in from Roundstone. I should be there in about twenty minutes."

"OK. Well, when you get here could you pop up to see me?" Hays said.

"Yeah, sure. What's up?"

"I'll tell you when I see you."

"OK. Sounds a bit ominous. See you soon!" Lyons said.

* * *

When Lyons got back to Mill Street Garda station, she went directly upstairs to Superintendent Mick Hays' office. She said hello to his personal assistant who was seated, as usual, at her desk outside his office.

"Go on in, Inspector. He's expecting you," the woman said.

Lyons did as she was told. When she entered the room butterflies were beginning to flutter in her stomach. It wasn't like her partner to be elusive, and she wondered what was coming. Had she screwed up somewhere along the line, or perhaps she had missed something very obvious that she was going to be informed about?

"Hi, Maureen. Come in, love. Grab a seat. Coffee?"

"No thanks, Mick. Why all the mystery?" she said, sitting down.

"Ah, no mystery. Just something I didn't want to talk about over the phone. It's about Séamus."

"Oh?" Lyons said. She was surprised that Hays wanted to talk to her about her brother-in-law. Definitely odd, she thought to herself.

"Yeah. I did a bit of detecting. I called Dodd and asked him if he could get the low-down on how Séamus actually is. He called the cardiologist up at the hospital – apparently, they are golfing buddies. He came back to me an hour or so ago. Look, this is a bit awkward, but it seems Séamus isn't as well as we thought. They're going to have him back in a couple of weeks for a triple bypass. His arteries are in a bad way, it seems, and his heart is quite badly scarred from the heart attack."

"Shit! I wonder if Sheila knows the full story."

"I imagine so, but you know what she's like. She's always so positive, and she may not have wanted to worry you."

"You're probably right. But that puts a new perspective on things, for sure. I doubt if he will be able to keep up the farm after that. It's pretty major stuff," Lyons said.

"How do you want to play it with Sheila?" Hays said.

"I'll give her a call later when I've figured it out. I don't suppose you fancy taking three months off to become a farmhand?"

"Eh... no, you're all right thanks. I'll stick to a nice warm desk job if it's all the same to you."

"I thought you might say that. Listen, thanks for that – I think. Best to know the score anyway."

"No problem. How's the murder enquiry going?" Hays said.

"Very slowly. There doesn't seem to be any motive for the killing, but there's something out of kilter with the woman. She appears to have had some sort of clandestine life that no one knew about, least of all her parents. We're just trying to expose it now, whatever it is."

"That's often the way with these things. Anyway, I have every confidence you'll crack it before too long. Let me know if you need anything, won't you?"

"Yes, of course. Right now, I could do with a hug."

Hays obliged and added a kiss or two for good measure before Lyons broke away and said, "I'd best be getting on. A killer to catch and all that!"

* * *

When Lyons got back to her own office, she called in John O'Connor.

"Hi, John. Did you get Aoife Gilpin's records from the post office?"

"Yes, I did. There's something very odd about them. Why don't I go and get the statements and show you?" he said.

"OK."

O'Connor was back a few moments later clutching a sheaf of A4 pages. He spread three of them out on Lyons' desk facing her. Some of the rows were highlighted in yellow, and he pointed to those entries.

"These are her wages going in from the hotel every week. Looks like she was on very little money in terms of actual pay. I calculated it to be somewhere around five-fifty or six euro an hour. But then there's these other lodgements too. Every week she seems to have deposited three or four hundred euro over and above her pay. She's worked up quite a nice little sum for herself. She has just over twelve thousand in her post office account."

"How long have these additional payments being going in?"

"They're not consistent. They seem to peak in the high summer and then tail off. But it's been going on for quite a while anyway."

"So, where do you think these extra sums have come from? Maybe tips from the hotel?" Lyons said.

"It's too much for that. Didn't one of the other girls say they sometimes get as much as €50 a week in tips, not hundreds?"

"Yes, you're right. So maybe sweet innocent Aoife had some other sort of sideline going. Any ideas?"

"No, none. She might possibly have been on the game, but I honestly doubt it. And someone would know about it if that were the case, I'm sure," O'Connor said.

"More bloody mystery. Speaking of which, any sign of the BMW driver popping up anywhere?"

"Not yet, I'm afraid."

"OK, John. Well, thanks for that. Let me know when you've cracked her laptop. Any joy from her phones?"

"None. The Nokia has only been used for voice calls to another burner. A few calls a week in both directions, always the same number, and the calls last between seven and fifteen minutes. No text messages or voicemail. And I haven't managed to trace anything on her iPhone either. Sorry."

"Great! Another dead end! Unless… Tell you what. Give the airtime provider a good rattle. Lay it on a bit thick; you know 'this IS a murder enquiry', that sort of thing. See if they can come up with anything useful. Better still, have you any connections with any other techy-minded folks that might work for them?"

O'Connor was non-committal.

"I'll see what I can do, boss. Leave it with me."

"Thanks. I'll hang onto these for now."

Lyons stared at Aoife Gilpin's account statements trying to make sense of what she was looking at without success. Thoughts of her sister kept floating into her mind, which prevented her from concentrating. Interrupting her daydreaming, Sally Fahy knocked on her door and came into the office.

"Hi, Sally. Any news?"

"No, not really."

Lyons explained about the bank account and told her colleague what John O'Connor was going to do about the phones.

"It's not much to go on, is it?" Fahy said.

"Tell me about it. We're rightly stuck on this one, Sally. Any bright ideas?"

"OK. Well let's go over what we do actually know. This lassie who seems as if butter wouldn't melt, turns out to be pregnant. And not just that, but it looks as if she comes into Galway at least once a week, during which time she lodges unaccounted-for cash to her post office account. So, obviously, she has something going on that her folks don't know anything about. Anything else?"

"Yes, there is. I'm not happy about two other aspects of this. Firstly, her father is acting strangely. We need to find out a bit more about him for starters. And we need to track down Liz Faherty or whatever her name is," Lyons said.

"And?" Fahy said, realising that her boss had a little more on her mind.

"And, Sergeant Fahy, the bus depot?"

"The bus depot? What do you mean?"

"C'mon. We're going out."

Chapter Eleven

The two detectives left Mill Street Garda station on foot. They crossed over the River Corrib into Bridge Street and on into Mainguard Street and then to the railway station and bus terminus at the corner of Eyre Square.

It didn't take Lyons long to find a Bus Éireann inspector. She approached, holding up her warrant card for the man to see.

"Good afternoon, may I ask your name?"

"Larry. Larry Egan. How can I help you, ladies?" Egan said cheerfully.

"My name is Senior Inspector Lyons, and this is Sergeant Fahy," Lyons said, gesturing towards her companion. "We'd like to talk to you about the bus service that comes in from Roundstone, particularly on Saturdays."

"Fair enough. What do you want to know?" the man said, looking a bit puzzled.

"Tell me, Larry, would it be the same driver that has the bus on most Saturdays on that route?"

"Let me see. Aye, I suppose it would. There are two services from Clifden via Roundstone to Galway on a Saturday. One in the morning and one just after lunch.

The same driver does the two, and that's him done for the day then."

"And who is that, usually?" Lyons asked.

"There are two different men do that route, unless one of them is off sick. There's Dinny Molloy and Bart Keegan."

"And where would we find Dinny and Bart, Mr Egan?"

"Ah, you'll not get them today. It's their day off. We have relief drivers on for their routes. But Dinny is on earlies tomorrow. He'll be taking the Westport bus out of here at nine-thirty. It goes all around the world for sport on its way to Roundstone that one, so he'll be at it all day."

"And what about the other driver – Bart, did you say?"

"Yes. Oh, I think he's on the Kilrush and Ennis route tomorrow. Let me just check."

Larry Egan took a thick dog-eared notebook out of the inside pocket of his coat, licked his thumb and turned the pages till he found what he was looking for.

"Aye, there you go. Galway to Kilrush. Leaves here at nine-forty all being well, and gets back here coming up to four in the afternoon, if there are no delays."

"How much in advance do the drivers usually arrive here at the bus station, Mr Egan?" Sally Fahy asked.

"Ah. You know how it is. They usually like to get a coffee and maybe a snack for the journey, and exchange a bit of banter with the other drivers, so I'd say about half an hour before the off. Dinny sometimes gets here a bit earlier. He has no one at home, you know, so he often gets a bit of breakfast up at the station. But what's all this about, Inspector?"

"We just need to ask them a few questions about the Roundstone bus, that's all. We won't delay them," Lyons said.

"Fair enough. You'll have to excuse me now, ladies. I have to get the express to Dublin away."

"Fine, thanks for your time."

Larry Egan strolled off towards one of the big red and white coaches with 'Dublin' indicated in an illuminated orange display over the windscreen. He officiated as the last few passengers boarded, the luggage doors were closed, and with a bit of hissing and a puff of black diesel smoke, the vehicle departed.

"OK, Sally. Let's you and me come down here tomorrow at around half-eight and talk to these drivers. Which one do you fancy?" Lyons said.

"I doubt if I'd 'fancy' either, boss. Let's see tomorrow. But what are you hoping to get from them anyway?"

"I don't know. But they may have seen Aoife with someone on the bus, or being dropped off or even meeting someone here. And when we get back to the office, I want you to see if Mary found anything on this Liz Faherty connection. We need to find her."

* * *

When Lyons got back to the station she went into her office and closed the door. She unlocked her PC and saw that there were a few emails that could probably wait till tomorrow for a reply. She spent a few minutes rehearsing what she would say on her next phone call.

"No point putting it off any longer," she said to herself. She lifted the phone and dialled her sister.

"Hi, Maureen," Sheila said as soon as she answered the call.

"Hi, Sheila. Is this a good time?"

"Yeah, sure. What's on your mind?"

"Listen, Sheila, I need you to be really honest with me on this. How is Séamus, really?" Lyons said.

There was a poignant silence from Sheila for a few moments.

"Damn! Who told you?" Sheila said, but not in an angry manner.

"Well, I am a detective, but that doesn't matter. Listen, how serious is it?"

"It's pretty bad. We've been told that he'll have to adopt a more sedentary lifestyle. I guess that's code for no more lugging huge bags of animal feed and heavy fencing posts around. It's a bummer, cos Séamus is a manual labour sort of guy. He loves all that stuff," Sheila said.

"Have you had a serious talk with him about it?"

"Not really. He says he will sit down with me when it has sunk in, but we've decided to put off the serious discussion till after his operation. In the meantime, he's taking it easy. He's been quite unwell for a while, but he's managed to keep it from me. You know what men are like. He's been dizzy and breathless quite often, and he's had to stop and take frequent breaks when he's been out working the land. That's not like him, and of course he never said anything or let on."

"God, I'm sorry, Sheila. Is there anything at all either Mick or I can do? Mick is very keen to help if he can, but having said that, he's no farmer!"

"It's OK. We've put some measures in place. The lads from down the road are happy to help, and Séamus has agreed some form of payment for them. He insisted. And the kids are great. But longer term, I'd like to have a chat with you about our options. But it's all a bit raw just now."

"OK. Of course. I understand. But whenever you want to talk, just call me. I'm here for you, you know. And try not to worry. It's great that it's been discovered before he had a really bad attack. And you know we'll support both of you whatever you decide."

"Thanks, sis, that's good to know. Now I'd better go and get the tea organised. At least Séamus hasn't lost his appetite!"

"OK. Talk soon. Bye."

* * *

Lyons was getting ready to leave the office, feeling quite frustrated with the lack of progress, when Sally Fahy came in.

"Hi, Sally. I hope you've got some good news for me."

"Well, kinda. There are twenty-eight people on the voters' register with Liz, Elizabeth or Lizzy Faherty or O'Flaherty in Galway. Now we've filtered the details by date of birth, and got a listing for all those between the age of eighteen and thirty. That narrows it down to twelve."

"Good work, Sally. Have you got the list there?"

"It's at my desk. Would you like a copy?"

"Yes please. And who have we got that could go and check these out? I'd prefer if it wasn't uniformed officers. We don't want to scare the daylights out of them."

"Well, maybe you and I could do it after we've finished with the bus drivers. Most of the addresses are all close to the city, except for two. One has an address in Louisburgh, and the other is from Carna. We could get Séan Mulholland to check those out. If we took five each it wouldn't take too long."

"Sounds like a plan. Can you set it up, but make sure Séan doesn't give them any advanced warning? There may be nothing in it anyway. We don't know if this Liz or Lizzy is material to the case," Lyons said.

"Yes, OK. I'll put that together now and give Clifden a call. Are you OK, boss?" Fahy asked.

"Yes. Why do you ask?"

"Ah, it's nothing. You just look a bit tired, that's all."

"Tell you what. When you've finished prepping the boys out in Clifden, let's go and get a drink somewhere. I could do with some advice in any case."

"OK, you're on. Give me twenty minutes."

Lyons used the time to inform Mick Hays that she would be going for a drink with Sally Fahy after work, and asked if they could meet up somewhere at around seven for something to eat.

"Sure, and bring Sally along too if she wants to. She's good company."

"Fine. I'll give you a call when we're ready to eat."

Sally Fahy was a very pretty blonde woman, and a very competent police officer. She had proven her worth several times over, but Maureen Lyons couldn't help but wonder if Mick Hays fancied her a little. She wouldn't blame him if he did. There had never been any signs that he had been unfaithful since Lyons and himself had got together some five years previously. They had been on a trip to Poland when they were investigating the murder of a young woman on the old bog road near Ballyconneely. But Lyons kept her antenna tuned all the same, and resolved to smarten herself up a bit with a trip to the hairdresser and maybe some new clothes to keep her man interested.

Chapter Twelve

Lyons and Fahy left the office and walked through the early evening crowds as far as Shop Street to their favourite watering hole. It was a busy place, but they were known to Peter, the proprietor, and he usually managed to find them a table near the back of the premises that afforded some privacy, as most of the patrons were clustered around the bar at this time of day.

When they were seated, Peter, dressed in a smart blue suit and pale button-down shirt approached.

"What can I get my two favourite detectives this evening?" he asked, smiling broadly.

"Hi, Peter. I hope you have a nice bottle of chardonnay keeping cool for us somewhere," Lyons said.

"But of course. Will you need a menu as well?"

"Not yet, in any case. Maybe in a while."

"Excellent. One bottle of delightfully cool chardonnay coming up," he confirmed as he swept away to fulfil their order.

Fahy was the first to open the conversation. "So, what's the craic?"

"Ah, nothing too serious. This case is doing my head in. We have absolutely bugger all on Aoife Gilpin, and

Mick is getting restless. He knows if we don't have some kind of breakthrough soon, Plunkett will be on his case, and there will be all the usual bullshit about getting the heavy mob from Dublin in to 'help' us. As if that would make any difference," Lyons said.

"Ah, don't mind them. It's all bluff anyway. They're always at that nonsense, but they've never acted on it. Not unless you count that prick that rummaged through my handbag that Mick had to see off."

"God, yes, I remember that. Speaking of which, how is the love life anyway?" Lyons said.

"Jesus! I don't know, Maureen. Kevin seems to be blowing hot and cold all the time. Some days he's all over me, then he vanishes for a week at a time and I don't even get a phone call. I can't figure him out. But I'm getting a bit fed up with his antics," Fahy said.

"Are you good together, you know?" Lyons said with an impish smile.

"Oh, yeah, no problem there, but I can't be doing with all this cloak and dagger stuff."

"He probably has a wife and six kids somewhere over near Portumna, or somewhere. Have you looked him up on the system?"

"No. To be honest I couldn't be arsed. If he's not fully committed, I don't really want it to go any further. Anyway. Enough about me. What about you?" Fahy said.

Lyons explained about her brother-in-law's condition, and her concerns for how it might change her sister's lifestyle permanently.

"It's tragic really. Sheila loves the country life and the farm and all that. It's hard work, but she's always been mad about it. When we were kids, she was always out across the fields with Dad doing something unspeakable with cow manure or something while I was in my room reading Enid Blyton books."

"Will they have to sell up?" Fahy said.

"I'm not sure how it will go. We're going to have a family powwow when Séamus has recovered from his triple bypass, see what we can figure out."

"Of course, you have an interest in the farm, haven't you?"

"Yeah, strictly speaking I own half of it, but I'm not that bothered, to be honest. It's really Sheila and Séamus's and they've been very generous to me anyway. That's how I was able to buy those apartments Mick and I own down near the docks."

"Cripes, yes, I'd forgotten about that. Are they doing OK – the flats, I mean?"

"Yeah, great. No bother. We have them more or less paid off now, so it will be handy money when we retire," Lyons said.

"God! Listen to you. You'll never retire, Maureen Lyons. You're too much of a cop for that. I can't see you at home growing sweet pea and pruning the roses while the scumbags of Galway are out and about creating mayhem!"

The two women laughed out loud.

* * *

The following day, Lyons was at her desk by eight o'clock. When Mick Hays had called to say he was ready to go and eat the previous evening, Sally Fahy had declined Maureen's invitation, not wanting to play gooseberry. In any case, she was going to try and track down her elusive boyfriend and issue a bit of an ultimatum to him.

Fahy arrived soon after eight, and herself and Lyons set off for the bus station to talk to the two drivers. It was a cool but fine morning in Galway, and the detectives elected to walk to the depot. They found the two men in the cafeteria at the railway station. Dinny Molloy was seated before what was left of a full Irish breakfast, while his companion, Bart Keegan, just had a large mug of strong tea.

Lyons had arranged that she would talk to Molloy and Fahy would see what Bart Keegan had to say. Fahy was able to remove Keegan from the table easily enough, and the two wandered off outside to have their talk, while Lyons sat down opposite Dinny Molloy.

"Dinny, I'm told you often drive the bus out through Roundstone to Clifden, is that right?"

"'tis, surely. I've been on that route now for nearly five years. I know it like the back of my hand," the man said.

Lyons took a photograph of Aoife Gilpin out of her pocket and unfolded it so that it was facing Molloy.

"Have you seen this woman on the bus at all lately?"

Molloy took a pair of spectacles out of the breast pocket of his jacket and put them on before studying the photo.

"I think that's one of the passengers that gets on near Roundstone, just before I get to the village on the way in from Clifden. I remember her, because she always has a suitcase with her, and the funny thing is, it's nearly always empty," Molloy said.

He removed his glasses, folded them, and returned them to his pocket.

"Empty? How do you know?"

"Well, on the way into Galway, she brings the case inside the bus and puts it in the overhead rack. If there was anything in it, she wouldn't be able to lift it up. It's quite awkward. But on the way back, she gets me to put the case in the luggage compartment, and then when we get to her place on the way back, I have to stop the bus, get out, open the side of the bus and lift it out for her. That's why I remember her so well."

"I see. So, let's get this straight. On the way into Galway, she has an empty suitcase with her, and on the way back, the suitcase has something in it. Have you any idea what?" Lyons asked.

"Not at all, girl. Sure what would I be doing nosing into someone's business."

"Did this happen every time Aoife got on the bus?"

"Yes, as far as I can remember. It's every second Saturday and Sunday, although sometimes Bart does the weekends, so you'd need to ask him as well."

"What kind of suitcase was it, Dinny?"

"Just ordinary. Like the kind of thing you'd take for a short week away or a long weekend. Not very big, but big enough, if you know what I mean."

"What colour was it?"

"Let me see. Eh... brown, I think. Yes, kind of dark tan, and quite well worn, but not broken or anything. That's all I can remember."

"Did Aoife meet anyone on the bus that you'd notice?"

"No. She nearly always sat in the same seat about halfway down along on the outside row. But I never seen her talking to anyone."

"And did she always get on and off at the same place, Dinny?"

"Yes, she did. She always went all the way to the depot here in town, and always boarded just outside Roundstone by that bungalow with the fabulous view out over the beach."

"OK, thanks, Dinny. That's been very helpful."

"What happened to the poor lass, anyway?" Molloy said.

"That's what we are trying to find out, Dinny. You'll have seen in the papers that she was killed. But we don't know by whom, or why, yet."

"It's a shame. She was a bonny lass."

* * *

When Fahy and Lyons got back together they compared notes. Bart Keegan had told exactly the same story about Aoife's journeys to and from Galway, including the procedure with her suitcase which Keegan had described just like his fellow driver.

Lyons took out her phone and called Pascal Brosnan.

"Hi, Pascal. I need you to do something for me. Will either you or Mary go out to the Gilpins' house this morning and see if you can get hold of a smallish brown suitcase belonging to Aoife. If it's there, use gloves and don't handle it too much. I want it brought in to Sinéad Loughran for analysis."

"Eh... OK. What will I tell the parents?"

"I dunno. You'll think of something. Just get it in here to the lab as soon as you can, OK?"

"Yes, OK. I'll let you know when we have it," Brosnan said.

When Brosnan had finished the call, he turned to Mary Fallon and relayed what Lyons had said.

"That's OK. I'll do that. I'm getting on fairly well with the mother. I'll make some excuse and get her to give me the case. Anyway, I could do with a trip into Galway. I need some new clothes."

"Oh, off you go then. Don't let a murder case get in the way of your wardrobe shopping," Brosnan said, but he was grinning broadly.

Chapter Thirteen

When they had finished at the bus station, the two detectives set off around the city to call on the addresses provided by the electoral roll for Liz or Elizabeth Flaherty. As they had arranged, they took five locations apiece, and agreed to meet up back at Insomnia Café on Eyre Square when they had finished. It turned out to be a thankless task. Lyons only managed to speak to the occupier at two of the houses. The other three were unoccupied, so she put a note in the door asking the homeowner to contact her as soon as they received it.

"How did you do?" Lyons asked when they were back together having a paper cup of soup and a rather hefty sandwich each in the café.

"Nothing. I got to speak to someone at each address, but none of them ever heard of Aoife Gilpin, and all of the Lizes seemed to be a good bit older than Aoife. What about you?" Fahy said.

"You did better than me. I only found someone in at two places, and same result. The first woman hadn't a clue what I was talking about. She goes by the name Betty, so the Elizabeth thing had her rightly confused. I left notes at the three where there was no reply. Maybe that will bring something?"

"Any word from the others out west?" Fahy said.

"No, not a peep. Maybe there'll be some news when we get back to the station," Lyons said.

"Let's hope so."

* * *

By mid-afternoon, Lyons was beginning to feel very despondent. She had been puzzling away at the scant information that they had on the case, and was thinking that they must have missed something crucial when her phone interrupted her thoughts.

"Lyons," she said.

"Hi, Maureen. It's Sinéad. Mary Fallon brought me in a present of a nice little weekend case. I'm all set for my next minibreak now! She said you'd asked her to collect it from the Gilpins' house."

"Yes, that's right. Have you had a chance to give it the once-over?"

"Yes, I have. There's not much to tell, to be truthful. Inside was very clean. There are no convenient airline labels on it anywhere, in fact no labels at all. But there is one thing that struck me as odd."

"What's that?"

"Was Aoife Gilpin a smoker?" Loughran said.

"I don't think so. Dodd would have mentioned it. Why?"

"Well, it's just that when I opened the bag up initially, I got quite a strong smell of tobacco. There was no residue anywhere in the bag. I checked the folds and the seams very carefully, but there was definitely a strong whiff."

"That's odd. Are you sure it was just tobacco, not anything else?"

"You mean like weed or something. No, it wasn't that. Pity we can't capture smells as evidence though, isn't it?"

"Hmm. OK. Well thanks for that. Anything else to report to cheer me up?"

"Hang on a minute. Yes, there is actually. One of the lads was working away on the polystyrene we recovered from the rubbish bags. He found a code number on one of the pieces and managed to trace it back. Apparently, it was used as packing for a Samsung TV, and not very long ago at that."

"Wow. How did he manage that?"

"It seems the plastic packaging industry has introduced measures to allow for the tracking of waste polystyrene, or EPS as we should be calling it. It's in response to fly-tipping, because most recycling centres won't take it. So, since last year there has to be a reference number moulded into the material, and you can use that to find out where it came from. The next step is to get the originators to pay for the removal and disposal of any that finds its way into fields, lay-bys or unauthorised dumps."

"God, Sinéad, you learn something new every day. Any way we can find out any more, like who the retailer of the Samsung device was?" Lyons said.

"No, not a chance. Unless we could get hold of the outer carton – the cardboard one. That would have all sorts of information on it, and it could be used to trace it back, no bother."

"Could you get your detective colleague to do a bit more digging for us, Sinéad?"

"Sure. How can we help?"

"Ask him to find out where household waste from the Gilpins' house would go and what happens to it for me, would you? I'm not sure if the council collect the bins there or whether the residents have to burn their rubbish, but it could be important."

"OK. I'll get back to you."

"Thanks."

When Lyons had finished the call with Sinéad Loughran, she called Mary Fallon's mobile, but it just went to voicemail. She left a message asking Mary to call her when she picked up.

Her humour wasn't much improved by her next call. Séan Mulholland rang in from Clifden.

"Hello, Maureen. I sent Jim Dolan out to those addresses you gave me for the Flaherty woman, but I'm afraid we drew a blank. Neither of them had heard of Aoife Gilpin, nor had any connection to the hotel in Roundstone or anything. Sorry," Mulholland said.

"Oh, never mind, Séan. That's the way the day is going for me. Thanks for trying anyway."

"No worries. Let us know if we can do anything more for you."

"Thanks, Séan."

More out of desperation than inspiration, Lyons went to find John O'Connor.

"Hi, John. Did you get a chance to do any background checks on Aoife Gilpin's father?"

"Yes, I did. It seems he works as a sort of financial advisor cum estate agent cum insurance broker. He has an office in Clifden over one of the shops there on Market Street. He calls it Equity Financial Services, but somewhat strangely, it's not a limited company, so the amount of financial information I can get about the operation is very limited. He just files abridged accounts that basically tell us nothing."

"Terrific. Have you been able to drill down into it at all?"

"Well, I can tell you there are no judgements against him or anything like that. He made a profit of forty-eight thousand odd last filing, but of course he could be taking a decent salary as well, and that level of detail isn't available in the Companies Office paperwork."

"OK. Well, that doesn't get us a whole lot further on, but thanks for your effort anyway, John."

Lyons went back to her office, more despondent than ever. She was still trying to make sense of it when Mary Fallon returned her call.

"Hi, Mary, thanks for getting back to me. I just wanted to ask you about the Gilpins' house. Do you remember being in the front room at all?"

"Yes, I was in there quite a bit early on when the news broke initially."

"Did you happen to spot what brand of TV they had there?"

"Oh, gosh, let me see. I think it might have been a Samsung, but I can't be completely certain. Why, is it important?"

"It could be. Any chance you could make up some story to visit the house again and confirm it for us?"

"Yes, I guess so. I'll drop in tomorrow morning. I'll say I just want to see how they are doing, and I'll make sure to check that out. I'll let you know."

"Thanks, Mary. Oh, and one other thing. Could you get Pascal to talk to the parish priest? I want to find out what type of family the Gilpins are. I know he won't divulge any detail about them, but just a few generalities will do for now. Pascal will learn more from the man's body language than what he actually says."

"OK. I'll ask him later on, and I'll call you tomorrow if there's anything new on the TV front."

"Great, thanks, Mary."

Chapter Fourteen

Lyons disliked it intensely when she was finding it hard to progress a case like this. It often got really in on her, and she became morose and sullen, which was not her natural state at all. She was normally bright and bubbly, but not at the moment.

When she got home, Hays recognised the symptoms.

"Hey, come here, you," he said, outstretching his arms and enveloping her in an affectionate hug.

He had the good sense not to say anything to try and cheer his partner up, but he held her close for quite a long time, and as he did so, he could feel the tension slowly draining from her body.

"Thanks, Mick," she said, withdrawing from the embrace.

"Right. Now, I'm afraid I haven't prepared a five-course gourmet dinner for my hardworking detective inspector, so any ideas? We could go out, or get food in, or you could shackle me to the stove if you're really feeling vicious!"

Lyons couldn't help herself. She just had to laugh.

"OK. You're on. Let's go out. You're the designated driver. I'm going to get pissed, and you're paying. How does that sound?"

"Pretty mean, to be fair, but depending on what's on offer for afters, I might just go along with it this once," he said with a sparkle in his eye.

"You'll be lucky, mate. C'mon, let's go."

* * *

The couple drove out as far as Pádraicíns Seafood restaurant in Furbo where they were assured of a sumptuous meal and some excellent wines. Lyons didn't in fact get drunk – it turned out to be all bravado on her part, and she didn't want to have a hangover the following day. But she did tuck into a delicious plate of fresh pan-fried scallops with a lemon cream sauce, followed by a very light lemon parfait, all washed down with a generous glass of chardonnay. By the time the meal was coming to an end, she was feeling more human.

"You're looking better now, Maureen. Feeling a bit more relaxed?" Hays said.

"Yes, thanks, Mick. I think you got this one just right!"

Hays blew on his fingernails and pretended to polish them on his jacket lapel.

"All part of the service, ma'am," he said smiling warmly. "Any news of Sheila?"

"Not today, but I'm going to call her in the morning and see if we can get together for a chat. She must be going through some kind of hell, although she conceals it well. Speaking of which, have you had your medical yet?"

"It's next month. But I'll be fine. I feel great these days."

"That's good. I don't want you keeling over on me – not yet anyway." She covered his hand with hers and stroked it gently.

Hays got the bill, as arranged, and left a decent tip for their waitress. He linked arms with Lyons as they walked to the car park, and opened the passenger's door first to let her in. Later, back at home, they spent an hour cuddling in front of the telly before heading upstairs for a sound night's sleep.

* * *

Lyon's body clock was programmed to wake her at 7:30 on weekday mornings, and when it came to the appointed hour, she awoke on cue. She could hear Mick in the shower. She spent a few minutes coming around, and when Hays emerged from the en suite, she hopped out to see to her own ablutions.

They had a quick breakfast of cereal and coffee, and then it was off to work for them both, in separate cars.

"Have a good one, love," Hays said as he gave her a kiss on the cheek in the hallway.

"Thanks, you too. I'll let you know when I've spoken to Sheila if there's any news."

"Yes, please."

* * *

Lyons had barely sat down at her desk when her landline rang.

"Inspector Lyons."

"Oh, hello, Inspector. My name is Izzy O'Flaherty. I got a call from my cousin late last night saying that you were looking for me."

"Yes, hello, Izzy, that's right. Firstly, can I just clear up something with you. Is Izzy your birth name?"

The woman at the other end of the call laughed briefly.

"No, it's not. I was christened Isobel, but when we were small my brother who is a year older than me couldn't manage 'Isobel' so he called me Izzy, and I guess it stuck. Everyone calls me Izzy or even Liz these days."

"Ah, thanks, that explains it. I believe you were friendly with Aoife Gilpin," Lyons said.

"Yes. That was dreadful what happened to her. Have you got anyone for it yet?"

"Our investigation is progressing. But listen, I'd like to meet you for a chat. Sometime today would be good. Can you come into the station here at Mill Street?"

"No, I'm sorry, I'm at work all day. I work at Lydon's on Buttermilk Walk, just off Middle Street. But if you came down here at about half past ten, I could take a break then and we could have fifteen minutes. Would that be OK?" Izzy O'Flaherty said.

"Yes, OK. I'll see you then."

"OK, thanks."

When Lyons had finished the call, she went to find Sally Fahy who was seated at her desk in the open plan.

"Sally, can we have a word in my office?" Lyons said.

"Sure. Coffee?"

"No thanks. It's a bit early for me."

When they were seated in the office, Lyons brought her colleague up to date with the phone call that she had taken from Isobel O'Flaherty.

"Do you think she'll have anything useful to tell us, boss? I presume you'd like me to tag along?" Fahy said.

"Oh, yes, please. I'm not sure. She's the only link we have to whatever Aoife was up to in the city, so I'm hoping she will have some useful information for us. Did John get anything useful from her PC?"

"I'm not sure. I'll check with him before we go out."

"OK. See if we have anything on the girl now that we know her real name. I have a few calls to make and then we'll head down town to see her."

When Fahy had left the office, Lyons called her sister.

"Hi, Sheila. How's things?"

"Hi, Maureen. Not great, to be honest. I can't say much just now. Do you think we could get together sometime soon for a chat?"

"Yeah, sure. Would you like me to come out there, this evening, maybe?"

"No. It would be better if we could meet somewhere away from the farm. I can come into town later for an hour or so if that would be good for you? It's only thirty minutes in the car."

"Yes, OK. If you don't mind the drive. What time suits?"

"Could we say around seven?" Sheila said.

"Great. Why don't you come to the station? There's plenty of privacy and parking, and I'm sure I'll still be here."

"OK. You're on, as long as you don't arrest me!" Sheila said with a chuckle.

"That, dear sister, depends on what you tell me! Go on. I'll see you later."

Chapter Fifteen

Buttermilk Walk is a narrow laneway that connects Middle Street and Saint Augustine Street in the centre of Galway city. Like much of the surrounding area, it is comprised of very old buildings, and some very new ones, or at least old ones that have been made new by development and refurbishment. Small cafés, pizza parlours, a Chinese takeaway, and even a tapas bar can all be found close by, reflecting Galway's multi-ethnicity, at least as far as food is concerned, that has developed in the last thirty years.

Lydon's offices occupy almost a third of the built space on the lane, and Lyons and Fahy found the entrance easily. Inside, the building was well appointed, and the receptionist greeted the two detectives professionally, asking them to wait in the comfortable reception area while she went to find O'Flaherty.

A few moments later, a short, thin woman with mousy dark blonde hair down to her shoulders and a pale complexion emerged from a doorway off the reception area. She was wearing blue denim jeans and a cream-coloured jumper with a cowl neckline and new-looking, smart trainers. She approached Lyons and Fahy.

"Hi. I'm Izzy. We can go out to the coffee shop for a few minutes if you like."

"Yes, OK," Lyons said, and the trio made their way out onto the street and walked a few metres back to Middle Street where there was a trendy café painted in fashionable grey with large lightbulbs with orange-coloured filaments suspended low over the black tables.

Inside, they took a seat in the window, and Sally Fahy went off to arrange refreshments.

"So, Izzy. Can you confirm that you were a friend of Aoife Gilpin, is that correct?" Lyons said.

"Yes. It's awful what has happened to her. Have you found out who did it yet?"

"Tell me, how did you two meet?" Lyons said, dodging the question.

"It's strange really. We were both at a book launch in Charlie Byrne's, and we got talking, and it went on from there. We liked the same kind of books, and we got on well from the start, so we met up when she came into town at the weekends," Izzy said.

Fahy returned with three very overpriced coffees and sat down.

"Did Aoife stay with you when she was in Galway?" Lyons asked.

"Yes, sometimes, but not always. Sometimes she got the bus back to Roundstone on Saturday evening, but she quite often stayed over."

"And did you ever go out to Roundstone and stay with the Gilpins?"

Izzy O'Flaherty looked down at her feet before answering.

"Just once," she said quietly.

"Oh. Was there a problem?" Fahy said, picking up on the girl's changed demeanour.

"Well, I shouldn't say anything really, but yes, I was uncomfortable."

"Why was that, Izzy?"

"It's probably nothing, but I was in the loo early on the Sunday morning, just having a pee. The bathroom door has no lock, and, well, as I was sitting there, Mr Gilpin came into the room. It was very awkward."

"What happened?" Lyons said.

"He came right into the room and had a good look at me. I had a loose-fitting sloppy T-shirt thing on, and I'm sure he could see everything. He never said sorry. Just had a nice long look and then left again. And afterwards, I think someone had been through my overnight bag. It was horrible."

"Did you say anything to Aoife?" Fahy said.

"No. I was too embarrassed, and anyway, he would just have said that it was a mistake, but I'm pretty sure it wasn't."

"What did Aoife do in Galway at the weekends, anyway, Izzy?"

Izzy looked down again, and she lost eye contact.

"Just shopping and stuff," she said, rather unconvincingly.

"What sort of 'stuff'?"

"Look, it's none of my business. I don't want to talk about it. And anyway, I don't really know anything."

"Izzy, if you want us to catch whoever murdered your friend, you need to tell us anything you know. Did Aoife meet anyone else here in town at the weekends?" Fahy said.

"Maybe. I can't really say."

"Well, did you two hang out together or what?" Lyons said, becoming a little impatient with the young woman's recalcitrance.

"I told you. I don't know anything. And anyway, I have to be getting back to work," Izzy said.

Lyons looked at Fahy, and shook her head imperceptibly.

"OK, Izzy. Well thanks for talking to us. If you think of anything else that might be relevant, please give me a call at any time. Here's my number," Lyons said, handing her a business card.

Izzy O'Flaherty looked very relieved that they were happy to end it there. She got up, thanked them for the coffee, and marched out of the coffee shop briskly, leaving Lyons and Fahy to themselves.

On the way back to the station, Lyons asked Fahy what she thought of the encounter.

"I'm not sure," Fahy said. "I kinda got the impression that she had rehearsed that story about Gerald Gilpin a bit too much. And she definitely knew more about Aoife's visits to Galway than she was letting on. But I don't think we could have got much more out of her today, in any case. What do you think?"

"I think you're exactly right. I'm sure we'll be talking a bit more to Miss Isobel O'Flaherty in due course, as soon as we know a bit more about what's been going on. But I also think we need to investigate Aoife's father a bit too. There may be something in what she said."

"I agree."

Back in Mill Street, Lyons approached John O'Connor.

"Sorry to interrupt, John. Look, I think we need to do a bit more digging on Gerald Gilpin. Can you do a thorough background check on the man and see what you can find? We'll be having a briefing later on."

"Yes, sure, boss. No problem."

The afternoon dragged on slowly. Midway through, Mary Fallon phoned in from Roundstone confirming that the television in the Gilpins' house was indeed made by Samsung.

"Mrs Gilpin said they got it when broadband hit the place a few weeks ago."

"Thanks, Mary. Is there any word on the bins?" Lyons asked.

"Bins? Sorry, I don't follow."

"I was asking Pascal to find out what happens to the domestic rubbish at the Gilpins'. I don't know if it's collected or if they have to dispose of it themselves."

"Oh, OK. Hang on, I'll ask Pascal."

Lyons could hear the exchange between the two Gardaí, and moments later, Mary Fallon came back.

"Pascal says that the rubbish is collected. There's a company called Bearna Waste Disposal that lifts the bins, and it's all supposed to be segregated into black, brown, and green."

"Ah, OK, Mary, thanks, that's what I was looking for. Talk soon. Bye."

Before the briefing got underway, Lyons reverted to her old practice of creating a spider diagram of the case. Aoife Gilpin was in a circle at the heart of the diagram, and lines spread out from the centre to 'Galway', 'Izzy O'Flaherty', 'Gerald Gilpin', 'Pregnant'; 'Black sacks'; 'Bertraghboy Bay Hotel' and 'Suitcase'. She stared at the diagram for some time, but nothing inspirational occurred to her.

In frustration, she got up, put on her jacket, left the building and went for a walk around the block to try and clear her head. But as she tried to figure out what had happened to the poor woman innocently on her way to work early in the morning, thoughts of her sister and her husband kept interrupting.

"Damn," she said to herself, "I'm going to have to ask Mick for help on this one, and I shouldn't have to. What kind of a detective am I?"

To add to her downbeat mood, the weather had turned, and it was starting to drizzle as she completed the circuit that had taken her across the River Corrib, over as far as Father Griffin Road and then into Dominick Street and back to the Garda Station. When she got back to her desk, she reluctantly called Mick Hays.

"Hi. It's me. Any chance you could spare me a few minutes?" Lyons said.

"Sure. Want to pop up?" Hays said.

"Thanks, I'm on my way."

* * *

Hays was busy poring over some report or other that had been sent down from Dublin, but when Lyons came into his office, he put it aside and gave her his full attention.

"Thanks, Mick. Sorry to bother you, but I'm at my wits' end with this Gilpin case. Any ideas?"

"What have you got so far?"

Lyons spread her spider diagram out for him to study, and talked him through it.

"Right. Well, the key here is motive. As I see it, there are two possibilities. Either it was because she was pregnant, or it's something to do with whatever was going on in Galway. You need to find out who the father of her unborn child is."

"Yeah, but that's not going to be easy. Her parents had no idea she was pregnant, and there's no one else saying anything. It could be anybody," Lyons said.

"So, why aren't people talking to you?" Hays said.

"I dunno. Scared, maybe."

"But scared of what, or who?"

The two of them said nothing for quite a few minutes.

"Tell you what, Maureen. Why don't you spend some time out there in Roundstone? You know how it works. The place sort of speaks to you. It worked for you before when that Polish girl was murdered out at Ballyconneely, and on other occasions too. Stay out there for a few days if you like. I can come out in the evenings to keep you out of mischief – it could be fun," Hays said.

"That's not a bad idea. I wonder if the Bertraghboy Bay Hotel is open again. I could stay there and make a right old nuisance of myself."

"That's the spirit. Better let Séan know what you're up to though. It is sort of his patch."

"Yes, I agree. But he won't make a fuss. Oh, by the way, Sheila is coming in later for a chat. I'm meeting her after work, so I'll be late home," Lyons said.

"Oh, right. Do you need me to sit in?"

"Best not this time. I'm not trying to exclude you, Mick, but I have a feeling she needs to get a few things off her chest woman to woman. Later on, we will need your help, for sure, if things go the way I suspect they will."

"I understand. Well, I'll be on standby if you do need me."

"Great. And thanks."

Chapter Sixteen

The team came together at five o'clock in the open plan on the detectives' floor at Mill Street. Lyons sat at the front of the little group, and gave a summary of what they knew to date.

"So, I have decided that I'm going to spend a few days out in Roundstone to see if I can get some kind of breakthrough with this lot. That doesn't mean you can all down tools here. There's plenty for you to be getting on with as well. But first, John, did you do a bit of digging on Gerald Gilpin?"

"Yes, I did, boss. It's very interesting. Gilpin was a secondary school teacher up to about eight years ago. He taught maths and science at Árd Scoil Naomh Brigid on the other side of town. He left suddenly, mid-term, it seems, and there's almost nothing about him on the school's website," O'Connor said.

"I see. Is that a mixed school?"

"Yes, it is," Eamon Flynn volunteered, "my nieces go there. It caters for boys and girls aged eleven to eighteen. It has a pretty good record too – academically, I mean. Not so good with sports, but not awful either."

"Interesting. OK, Eamon, seeing as you have connections there, can you contact them and find out why Gilpin left so suddenly mid-term, and let me know what you find out. OK?"

"Yes, boss."

Fahy updated the team on the conversation that had taken place with Izzy O'Flaherty too.

"We need to probe this one a bit further. Izzy has a lot more to tell us. I'm going to call at her workplace again tomorrow and put a bit of pressure on her, see what I can squeeze out of her," Sally Fahy said.

"And, John, can you get onto Bearna Waste and find out what days they collect the rubbish from Aoife Gilpin's house?" Lyons said. "And see how long they keep paper waste for and what they do with it as well, will you?"

"Yes, OK. What are you thinking, boss?"

"I am thinking, John, about the polystyrene that was in the rubbish bags that caused Aoife Gilpin to stop her bike just where she was attacked. Where did it come from? How did it get there? Who handled it? And if we can find the carton that the Samsung TV came in, we might just be able to trace the stuff back to source. Get it?"

"Yes, I see where you are coming from. But didn't Mary say that the Gilpins had a new Samsung TV?" Sally Fahy said.

"Yes, but I understand that broadband has just been made available out that way, so several households may have upgraded their telly to take advantage. So, while we are at it, I'll get Séan Mulholland to talk to the electrical shop in Clifden and see if he can find out anything, though some folks may have come into Galway to make their purchases."

With the meeting over, Lyons phoned the Bertraghboy Bay Hotel. She learned that it had in fact reopened, and she booked herself in for three nights dinner, bed and breakfast starting the following evening. Then she telephoned Séan Mulholland and told him of her plans.

"That's great, Maureen. Maybe I'll drop over one of the nights and we can have a drink together. Will the superintendent be with you?"

"I'm not sure yet what his plans are, Séan, but it doesn't make any difference anyway, I'd be glad to see you. Will you tell Pascal and Mary for me?"

"I will, to be sure. I'll talk to you tomorrow so."

"Right, Séan, thanks."

* * *

Sheila arrived at Mill Street Garda station at just after seven o'clock that evening. The officer on the front desk called up to Lyons who was in her office dealing with the crop of emails that had arrived during the day. She went downstairs and collected her sister, taking her to one of the more comfortable interview suites that was designed to make you feel less like a criminal.

"Thanks for this, Maureen. I'm sorry to take up your time. I know you're busy with this Gilpin thing. How's it going anyway?"

"Ah, ye know. To be honest, it's driving me mad. But listen, you didn't come all the way in here to talk about that. Do you need a coffee or something? I think I could rustle it up, but it won't be very Café Sol, or Insomnia."

"No, thanks. I'm fine."

"So, what's the story with Séamus?"

"Well, we had a long talk with the cardiologist the other day. I'm afraid it's not very good news. To make a long story short, it looks as if we may have to give up the farm," Sheila said.

"Cripes! That's dreadful. Maybe Séamus could get someone else to do the heavy work, and leave him just sort of supervising, or something?" Lyons said.

"No, that's not an option. Firstly, the farm wouldn't be viable under that arrangement. It's doing OK now, but that's because Séamus puts in the work of two or three men. Don't get me wrong. He loves it, but that's the reality of it. And secondly, Séamus just couldn't do that. He's a real hands-on kinda guy. He'd never be able to watch someone else doing it. It would drive him into an early grave."

"Hmm... I see. So have you got a plan?"

"Well, sort of. That's why I wanted to talk to you, cos you have a half interest in the place."

"Oh, don't worry about that, sis, I'll go along with whatever you decide. As far as I'm concerned, it's your business, and I've already had a good few bob out of it. That's what allowed me to buy the apartments down by the docks with Mick."

"I know. But we still need to talk. The thinking at the moment is that we could sell off most of the land. Séamus said we could let around 100 acres go, and still keep enough around the house to have a few pigs and hens to stop him going completely crazy," Sheila said.

"And what would that fetch, Sheila?"

"Séamus has done a bit of research. He says what with the road frontage and all on the east side of the farm, and the hay barn he built a few years back, it should be worth about €8,000 an acre or maybe a bit more. He has kept it in very good condition, you know, and it's all quite flat."

"That's a small fortune! Any idea what you would do with the money?"

"Well, of course, half of it would be yours, and then we'd have to spend a bit on setting up the piggery and buying stock, but we'd probably get a good lot for the cattle too, so we'd be left OK, I guess. But what would you think of us selling off the land that Dad built up over the years through the sweat of his brow?"

"I don't have any sentimental attachment to it, Sheila. We have to deal with the circumstances we find ourselves in today, and Dad would be the first to recognise that. He was very pragmatic. If that would mean that Séamus could take it a good deal easier, and still be occupied, then it's fine by me."

"Do you not have to talk to Mick about it?" Sheila said.

"Well, I'll tell him of course, and he may even have a few ideas about your situation, but he'll respect the fact that it's my decision. He's not my boss at home!"

"God, that's great, Maureen. I thought you might be horrified at the thought of losing the place. But listen – there's something else. I don't want us to get ahead of ourselves, but if the plan worked out, we'd have quite a decent lump sum from which we would need to generate income. We were wondering if Mick and yourself could give us some advice on that? Neither of us have a clue."

"We're not exactly business people either, Sheila. But we'd be happy to give it a bit of a rattle and see what we could come up with. My immediate thought is property. We get a couple of thousand a month from the place I used to live in and those apartments we bought which comes in very handy. But Séamus might have different ideas. How much do you need to run the house and that?"

"We haven't worked it out properly yet. The farm outgoings and the household costs are all mixed up, so we'd need to go back over the figures and see exactly how much it costs to run the house. But at a rough guess, I'd say between two and three thousand a month would do it."

"So, if you invested, say, €350,000, you'd be looking for a yield of around 10% after tax. That's a pretty tall order, Sheila. But listen, Mick knows more about these things. He'll probably have some ideas. How quickly do you want to move on this?" Lyons said.

"More or less straight away, but I wanted to talk to you first before we did anything decisive in case you objected to the whole thing."

"No, not at all. We have to do what's best for you both now. It will be a big enough wrench for Séamus as it is without me bleating on about it."

Sheila got up and came over to Maureen and gave her a long hug. When she released the embrace, Maureen could see that she had tears in her eyes.

"It will be OK, sis. You'll get through this. Trust me. And Mick and I will give you both all the support we can, have no fear on that score."

"Thanks, Maureen. It has been pretty tricky since Séamus had the heart attack. It's great to know that you're on our side. That means a lot. Is there anything I can do for you?" Sheila said.

"Not unless you can find me a murderer. But it's OK. It's just I hate it when things aren't moving along at pace, and this one definitely isn't."

The two sisters chatted on for another twenty minutes or so, and then Sheila left to drive back out to the farm near Athenry. Lyons collected her things and set off for home herself. She had a lot to talk to Hays about.

Chapter Seventeen

The next day was bright and clear, with just a few innocent-looking clouds tracking west to east across the countryside as Lyons drove out to Roundstone. She had packed a small suitcase with sufficient changes of clothes to do her in case she got soaked by one of the all too frequent showers. It was often said that Connemara could deliver all four seasons in the same day, on occasions.

She pulled her Volvo into the parking area in front of the little Garda station in Roundstone close to the Catholic church, and went inside. Both Pascal Brosnan and Mary Fallon were at their respective desks, and Brosnan got up when he saw Lyons coming in.

"Good morning, Inspector. You're out bright and early. Can I get you a cup of tea or coffee?"

"No thanks, Pascal. I just wanted to have a chat with you both before I go down to the hotel to check in. Anyway, I'm far too early for them, but I'm hoping to pay a courtesy call on Séan Mulholland later on in any case."

Lyons sat down on a spare chair positioning herself between the two Gardaí.

"OK, have either of you got anything more to report?"

Brosnan spoke up.

"Not much, Inspector. But there is one thing that has me a bit puzzled."

"Go on."

"Last night after work, I changed into casual clothes and went down to the hotel for a pint. I sat up at the bar. There were a few tourists in, and I got chatting to a Canadian bloke who was there with his wife doing the Wild Atlantic Way. They were staying a few nights. This fella was a smoker, and he went outside for a ciggy halfway through the conversation. When he came back in, his cigarette packet was empty, so he scrunched it up and threw it on the bar."

"So?" Lyons said, wondering where this was going.

"Well, yer man went off to bed at about quarter to ten. And then I was chatting to the barmaid that was serving. It was very quiet at that time. Just me and two others in the place. The empty fag packet the Canadian had discarded caught my eye. It wasn't one of the usual brands that you'd see in the shops here, so I picked it up. The brand was Dorchester, which I know you can't buy locally, and I looked it up this morning, and apparently, it's one of the most commonly smuggled brands in the country," Brosnan said.

"I don't suppose you managed to ask this guy where he got them?"

"No, but I noticed that the barmaid seemed quite nervous when she saw me taking the empty packet."

"Did you get her name?"

"Yeah, she's Stella. She sometimes works the desk at the hotel, but last night she was in the bar."

"But that guy could have got the cigarettes anywhere. Why do you think it might be connected to the hotel?"

Mary Fallon answered, sensing Brosnan was feeling a little uncomfortable.

"It's just that what with the evidence of Aoife's empty suitcase, and that, it may be that there's some kind of scam going on with smuggled tobacco products at the hotel, and that Aoife Gilpin was somehow involved."

"It's a bit of a leap, though. Pascal, have you any idea what the next stop on Canada-man's itinerary is?" Lyons said.

"He mentioned something about Kylemore Abbey. I think they may be going over there today on their way around."

"Good. Did you get his name?"

"Just his first name, it's Logan something or other."

"Did you see what kind of car he was driving?"

"No, 'fraid not, sorry."

"How strongly do you want to follow this, Pascal?" Lyons said.

"How do you mean?"

Fallon felt that there was some tension between the inspector and her colleague, so she intervened again.

"If you like I could call the hotel and see if he left a car registration number on his check-in document. And they might have some idea of his next stop too, and I could get his surname."

"Good idea, Mary. Yes, do that please. Pascal, can you get onto the lads in Letterfrack and see if they would have anyone available to drive out to Kylemore to have a chat to Logan or whatever he's called. Tell them we'll have more information about him soon."

While Lyons was waiting for Brosnan and Fallon to make their calls, she went outside and placed a call back into Mill Street where she spoke to Eamon Flynn.

"Hi, Eamon. Just wanted to see if you found out anything about Gilpin and the school. Any news?"

"Oh, right, boss. Yes, I did. They were a bit guarded about what they said, but reading between the lines, there was some likelihood of improper behaviour towards a teenage girl. The parents made a complaint, and although it didn't get very far, Gilpin left the school and that seemed to put the lid on it. I'm not sure if any money was handed over, but it wouldn't surprise me."

"I see. Any idea what he was supposed to have done?" Lyons said.

"He became quite attached to one of the kids. Her parents made a complaint, it seems. That's all the school would tell me, but they also took measures to ensure that he didn't work with kids again, so it was probably a bit more serious than they are letting on. What are you going to do about it, boss?" Flynn said.

"Nothing, for now. But I'm not going to forget about it either. Look, things are happening here. I'd better go. Talk later."

"Right, and we keep this to ourselves for now, OK?" Flynn said.

"Yes, of course."

* * *

When Lyons went back indoors, Fallon and Brosnan had finished their various phone calls.

"What's the story, folks?" Lyons asked.

"The Canadian is Logan Clarke. I got his car reg number from the hotel as well. It's a rented Skoda Fabia with a Europcar sticker in the back window," Mary Fallon said.

"And I've given the details to the Gardaí from Letterfrack. They're on their way out there now. Should be at the Abbey in about fifteen minutes. I've told them to put him at ease and just find out where he got the smokes, and if he has any more of them. I've asked them to get hold of the cigarettes if they turn out to be dodgy, but I don't think we want to prosecute Clarke, do we?" Brosnan said.

"No, you're right, we don't need that as long as we get a statement from him if he did buy them cheap at the hotel," Lyons said.

"Yeah. The guys are on it."

* * *

Kylemore Abbey was looking stunning as ever, bathed in sunlight, against the backdrop of the sheer mountain behind it. It wasn't very busy on this particular day, with just over twenty cars in the car park. The two Gardaí from Letterfrack drove around until they located the rental car with the registration number that they had been given.

"You stay here with the car, Jim. I bet the Clarkes are in the café or the shop. I'll be back in a few minutes."

"Righto," Jim said, as his colleague set off towards the expansive set of new buildings housing a large craft and souvenir shop and a good-sized restaurant. He had little difficulty locating his quarry, as they were the only couple seated, having coffee and scones, at one of the tables.

"Mr Clarke," the Garda said, approaching the table.

"Yes, that's right, how can I help you, officer?" Logan Clarke said.

"I wonder if I could ask you if you have purchased any cigarettes recently, sir?"

"Yes, of course," Clarke said grinning broadly, "though I'm surprised to be approached by a cop looking to cadge a smoke."

The Garda remained stony-faced, so Clarke had to continue.

"I bought a carton of 200 in the hotel that we stayed in last night. Why do you ask?"

"I wonder if I could see the pack please, sir?"

"Well, yes, I guess. But what's all this about, officer?" Clarke said, humour now having deserted him.

"If you could just show me the pack, please?" the Garda persisted.

"It's in my car out in the car park. Wait here, Maeve, I'll not be long," Clarke said getting up from the table and addressing his wife, who seemed completely disinterested.

The Garda and Logan Clarke walked silently to the back of the Skoda and Clarke opened the boot. He rummaged briefly in his luggage, and produced an open carton of Dorchester that had just two packs of twenty missing. He handed them to the Garda.

"I'm afraid these cigarettes are contraband, Mr Clarke. There's no Irish Government health warning on them, and that brand isn't sold in this country. Neither is there an Irish Government tax stamp on any of the packets," the Garda said.

"But that's impossible! I bought them at the hotel, from the woman at the bar. She'll tell you," Clarke said, becoming quite flustered.

"I'm sure she will, Mr Clarke, but it doesn't mean they are legitimate. I'm afraid I'm going to have to confiscate these, and any others you may have about your person."

"Are you serious?" Clarke said.

"Very."

Clarke reluctantly handed over the cigarettes and reached into his jacket pocket where he found an open packet that he also gave to the Garda. The entire lot was placed in an evidence bag.

"Now, Mr Clarke, my colleague here will just get some details from you if you don't mind. I don't think you'll be prosecuted this time, but we will need you to make a formal statement. As a matter of interest, how much did you pay the barmaid for them?"

"Let me see, eh, fifty euro I think, yes that was it."

"Hmm... that amount of cigarettes should have been at least three times that if they were tax paid. Did you not realise the price was a bit too good to be true?"

"No, no I didn't. I have no idea how much they should have been in Ireland. I normally buy my tobacco in Canada."

"And how much are cigarettes in Canada, Mr Clarke?"

"Oh, depending where you go, but usually around a hundred and fifty Canadian dollars for a carton this size."

The young Garda just gave the visitor a withering look.

While the second Garda was taking down Clarke's particulars from his passport, and finding out where his itinerary would take them over the next few days, his colleague called back to Roundstone. He spoke to Pascal Brosnan and relayed the information to him.

"That's great. Thanks for doing that. I'll pass it on to the inspector. Do you fancy a trip back to the station via Clifden? The boss has gone out there and she could collect them from you?"

"Ah, sure, why not. It's a grand day for a drive."

Chapter Eighteen

When Lyons had set things in motion in Roundstone, she set off for Clifden. The drive up past Dog's Bay and on out towards Murvey and Ballyconneely was very picturesque. Lyons always enjoyed this drive, even when the sun wasn't shining. There was something special about the air all along the Atlantic coast, so she lowered the windows to let the freshness circulate all around. As she passed the various dilapidated properties on the sea side of the road, her mind wandered back to the nineteenth century when Ireland was gripped by famine, and people moved to the coast to live off a meagre diet of fish and seaweed. By 1860, the population of the country had been reduced from over eight million twenty years earlier to just over five million by virtue of mass emigration and starvation.

Lyons arrived in Clifden soon after eleven and parked her car outside the Garda station at the start of the main Galway Road. Inside, Sergeant Séan Mulholland was just setting up his mid-morning cup of tea and a saucer of chocolate biscuits that was his any-time-of-day snack.

"Good morning, Maureen. I heard you were on the way out. Would you like a cup of tea?"

"Thanks, Séan, yes, that would be lovely."

Mulholland fetched another mug and prepared a drink for Lyons. As he placed it on the table, he nudged the saucer of biscuits in her direction, rather hoping she wouldn't take any.

When the two of them were settled at the table, Mulholland listened intently as Lyons brought him up to date with progress on the Aoife Gilpin murder.

"Do you know Gerald Gilpin at all, Séan?"

"Oh, that one. I do, to be sure. You know he used to be a teacher?"

"Yes, I knew that. It seems he was dismissed for inappropriate behaviour with one of the teenaged girls."

"And that wasn't the end of it. After he was let go, he started a business of sorts here in the town and he employed a young one. She only lasted a few weeks, and then she left abruptly. She never made a complaint or anything, but the rumours went around."

"Did you ever speak to the girl?" Lyons said.

"Ah, you'd see her out and about, but I never spoke to her about what happened with Gilpin. It would have been awkward to raise it with her if she just wanted to forget about it and move on."

"What did he do for an assistant then?"

"He employed Aoife for a while. But then she left too and went to work in the hotel in Roundstone. I don't think he has anyone working with him since. Once the word got out, none of the lassies from here would go near him. But what's all this about tobacco and cigarettes, Maureen?"

"We're just sorting that out now, Séan. But it looks like there's some kind of scam going on at the hotel involving the sale of contraband tobacco, and it appears that Aoife Gilpin may have been mixed up in it. But it's not clear exactly what it's all about just yet. That's why I've come out. I'm staying at the Bertraghboy Bay Hotel for a couple of nights to see what I can find out."

"Is there anything I can do?" Mulholland said.

"Hmm... maybe. Could you and some of the lads here visit each of the hotels and see if you can spot anyone with Dorchester brand cigarettes?"

"Oh, yes, that's no problem. I'll get Jim Dolan and Peadar to do the rounds, and see what they can find out, though I'd be surprised if there's any of that nonsense going on in the town. I'm sure one of us would have come across something."

"Thanks. And do you think it would be worth having a chat with the girl that used to work for Gilpin? She might open up to a female officer more easily."

"True. But it was a while since. I'm not sure it's worth opening up old sores."

"Maybe not. Let's leave it for today, anyway. We can come back to it if it seems relevant."

Mulholland was relieved. He didn't relish the thought of stirring up a hornet's nest.

"Do you think the murder has anything to do with the tobacco scam?" Mulholland said.

"Well, it's certainly a possibility. But there's some circumstantial linking Gilpin to it as well," Lyons said.

"God, I hope it's not that, Maureen. Such a thing would cause terrible unease in the community."

* * *

Lyons stayed chatting to Séan Mulholland for another while, and then left him to his own devices. She walked up along the main street and stopped into a newly decorated coffee shop, where she had a bowl of soup for an early lunch. She would have invited Mulholland to join her, but she didn't want to draw attention to the fact that she was with the Gardaí just yet. She wasn't well known in Clifden, and she wanted to keep it that way for now. After she had downed a delicious bowl of vegetable soup, made with real stock, and eaten the accompanying slice of multigrain bread, she set off back to Roundstone.

The place was very quiet when she arrived at the hotel close to three o'clock, and there was no one at reception. She had a quick look behind the desk to see if she could spot anything out of the ordinary, but it all seemed to be in order. When she came back around to the front of the desk, she saw a bell at the edge of the counter and gave it a push. After a moment, a young woman appeared.

"Hi. My name is Lyons. I have a reservation."

The receptionist produced a registration form that Lyons filled in, leaving out the fact that she was a serving Garda officer.

"Thanks. If you'd like to come with me. Do you need a hand with your luggage?" the receptionist said, helpfully.

"No, you're grand," Lyons replied.

Lyons was shown to room number four. It was spacious, with a bay window giving a side view of the sea down across the harbour in Roundstone village. Although the room was obviously part of the original building, and hence old, successful attempts had been made to modernise it. A good woollen carpet covered the floor, and the large double bed had a night locker on each side on which lamps with LED bulbs were positioned. On one side there was a modern telephone instrument. In the bay window, a low table was positioned with a flat screen TV. A door off the bedroom led into a smart en suite bathroom that had stylish pale beige floor-to-ceiling tiles and fashionable vitreous ware, along with a large square shower head suspended over the bath.

"Very nice. Sorry, may I ask your name?" Lyons said to the woman who was still standing just inside the door.

"Stella."

"Thanks, Stella. That's great. What time do you serve the evening meal?"

"Dinner is served between seven and nine. Would you like me to reserve a table for you?"

"Yes, please."

"Will you be on your own?"

Lyons smiled.

"Probably," she said, wondering if Hays might come out to join her.

When Stella had left, leaving the key to the room on the dresser adjacent to the door, Lyons unpacked her few belongings and put them in the wardrobe. She lay on the bed, and took out her mobile phone. She noticed that there was a small card on the nightstand informing guests that the Wi-Fi password for the hotel was 'BBH2018'. She keyed the not very imaginative code into her phone, and it immediately connected her to the world wide web.

Lyons scrolled through some of the latest news items, but after a few minutes she actually dropped off to sleep.

* * *

Lyons was awoken by the ringing of her phone, which lay on the bed beside her. She picked it up and looked sleepily at the screen. It was Mick Hays calling.

"Hi, Mick. Everything OK?"

"Hi, love. Where are you?"

"I'm in my room at the hotel here in Roundstone. What time is it?"

"Just after half past five. Why?"

"God, I must have dropped off. The air out here makes me sleepy."

"Sleeping on the job! That won't do at all, Inspector. Anyway, any news?"

Lyons told her partner about the information Séan Mulholland had given her on Gerald Gilpin.

"Interesting. And didn't you say Aoife Gilpin was expecting?"

"Yes, she was. But it's a bit of a leap to think her father might be involved, surely?" Lyons said.

"Tell you what. Why don't you see if you can get a sample of Gerald Gilpin's DNA? I think they can compare it to the DNA of the foetus and determine if her father was its father, if you see what I mean."

"Crikey! I'm not sure I like where this is going, Mick. And I don't know if he would be willing to give us his DNA in any case. What excuse could I use?"

"Just say it's connected to ongoing enquiries or some other bullshit. Get a sample from the missus as well to make it look more routine. Have you got a swab test thingy with you?"

"Yes, I have a few of them in the car. OK. Maybe that would work. Let me think about it for a while. Now, to more important matters. Would the superintendent by any chance be driving out in this direction tonight?" Lyons said.

"Aw, sorry, hun, I'm afraid I can't. I have to go to a meeting with his nibs later on. Some hot shot civil servants are down from the Department of Justice and they want to meet him, and he's not happy going on his own in case he gets bushwhacked."

"So, a poor lonely, sleepy, female officer has to stay all on her own in this fine big bed all night long then?" she said, lowering her voice to a sultry whisper.

"'fraid so. But you're there tomorrow night too, aren't you?" Hays said.

"Yes, but by that time I may have picked up a hunky farmer to keep me company."

Hays ignored the remark.

"Maybe I'll see if I can escape tomorrow then. I'll see how it goes."

"I suppose that will have to do. OK. I'd better go and have a shower. Enjoy your meeting with Plunkett. Love you."

"You too. See ya."

When Lyons finished the call, she phoned Roundstone Garda station. It was answered by Mary Fallon.

"Hi, Mary. It's Inspector Lyons. Listen, would you by any chance be able to stay on a bit this evening? There's a little job I have to do at around eight o'clock, and I'd like to have you with me."

"Yes, I guess that would be OK. What's the job?"

"I'll tell you later. Oh, and have you any civilian clothes with you?"

"Yes. I always keep a change here in the station."

"Great, well why don't you change, and come down to the hotel here for six-thirty, and we can have dinner together. Then we can go out on our mission."

"Eh... OK. See you soon."

Lyons called down to the front desk to alter her meal reservation, and then hopped in the shower for a long hot soak.

Chapter Nineteen

Lyons was sitting up at the bar nursing a soda water with ice and a slice of lime when Mary Fallon came into the hotel. She had changed into dark slacks, a cream blouse, and a pale pink jacket, and she looked fantastic with her blonde hair hanging loose around her shoulders. She spotted Lyons straight away, and joined her at the bar.

"Hi, Mary. Thanks for this. What can I get you?" Lyons said.

"Are we on duty?"

"Kinda. But have a drink if you want one."

"No, it's OK. I'll just have a tomato juice please."

The barmaid went off to get Mary's drink, and Fallon leaned in a little closer to Lyons and said, "What's going on, Inspector? Why all the secrecy?"

Lyons looked around to see that there was no one within earshot, and filled her colleague in on the latest information about the Gilpins.

"That's horrible. Do you think there may be something in it?" Fallon said.

"That's what we need to find out. I wasn't sure if what Mick had said about DNA was correct, so I looked it up on Google while I was waiting for you. Apparently, in an incestuous pregnancy, the DNA of the baby shows an 'absence of heterozygosity', whatever that is. But it's quite unambiguous. So, we need to get Mr Gilpin's DNA. When we've had our dinner, we can go out to the house and do the deed. I'll ask Mrs Gilpin for a sample too, and say it's just routine. Let's hope they buy it."

The two officers took their drinks into the dining room and sat at a table near the window. There were just a handful of other patrons in at this early hour, and when they were presented with menus, Lyons and Fallon were impressed by the selection and the descriptions on offer. Lyons chose a smoked salmon starter, followed by slow-cooked lamb shank with mashed potato and seasonal vegetables, while Fallon opted for country vegetable soup followed by pan-fried hake. They were not disappointed with the food. Both portions were generous, and cooked to perfection.

When they had finished eating, and were waiting for coffee, Lyons said to Fallon, "How are things going with Pascal, Mary?"

"Slowly. But that's the way I want it. We've been out together a few times, and we've kissed, but that's all. I'm not sure it's even a good idea, but I do like him, and he seems to like me too."

"As you know, I'm in no position to judge. Go with your instinct is what I'd say. Is he any good in bed?" Lyons said, looking directly at Fallon.

"God! I told you, boss, we haven't got that far. But he's a very good kisser!"

* * *

At quarter past eight, Lyons brought her Volvo to rest outside "Radharc na Farraige". Gerald Gilpin's enormous 4x4 was parked in the driveway.

"Now remember, Mary. This is no biggie. Just treat it as routine. We can swab the inside of their mouths. I have the kit here," she said, tapping the front of her jacket.

They got out of the car and knocked on the door. After a couple of minutes during which Lyons admired the amazing view there was from the front of the Gilpins' house, the door opened and Mrs Gilpin peered out.

"Good evening, Mrs Gilpin. I wonder if we could come in for a few minutes?" Lyons said.

"I suppose so. We're just finishing our meal," the woman said, standing aside and allowing them to enter.

Mrs Gilpin showed them into the room at the front of the house with the magnificent view, and said she was going to get her husband.

"What can we do for you, ladies?" Gerald Gilpin said as he entered the room, taking a good look at the junior officer. "Have you come to tell us who killed Aoife?"

"No, I'm afraid not, Mr Gilpin, but our enquiries are moving along."

"Hmph," he responded, sitting down on the sofa beside his wife who managed to look tense and timid at the same time.

"We just need to collect a DNA sample from you both, if that's OK," Lyons said.

"Whatever for?" Gerald Gilpin said.

"It's just routine in these cases. It may help us to advance our investigation. I'm sure you understand," Mary Fallon said.

"Well, if it will help you to find out what happened, I suppose it's OK, but I don't understand," Mrs Gilpin said.

"It's nothing to be concerned about, Mrs Gilpin. And it only takes a minute. We just need to swab the inside of your cheeks with this cotton bud thing," Lyons said, producing the kit.

"Look, is this really necessary? I mean, I've had a drink with my meal. Won't that corrupt the sample?" Gerald Gilpin said.

"No, not at all. It doesn't affect it," Lyons said, advancing on the man with the probe now unpacked. Before he could speak again, the thing was at his mouth, and he had little choice but to open it and allow the procedure to go ahead.

Mary Fallon did the same with Mrs Gilpin, and after another few minutes of general conversation, the officers got up to leave. There was no talk of Aoife's pregnancy at all. The only thing they wanted to know was when they could bury their daughter.

"It will be a little while yet, I'm afraid. But we'll let you know in good time to make the arrangements," Lyons said.

Outside and back in the car, Lyons said to Mary Fallon, "Mary, can you take these into Sinéad Loughran tomorrow morning. I'll square it with Pascal if necessary. Explain to Sinéad what they are about, and ask her to compare Mr Gilpin's sample to the DNA from the unborn baby."

"Yes, sure, boss. But I hope it's not what you think. That's disgusting."

"I know, but not entirely unheard of, I'm afraid. Especially out in the country. Look, why don't we go and get a proper drink. You can stay over at the hotel if you don't want to drive. I'm sure they'll have a spare room."

Lyons and Fallon went back to the hotel. They ordered proper drinks and sat in the bar talking for ages. Lyons kept a sharp eye out for any dodgy dealings in tobacco going on in the bar, but she saw nothing of interest.

At just after half past ten, Fallon's phone rang. It was Pascal Brosnan.

When she had finished the call, Lyons said, "He's keen."

"He's definitely a keeper. He's only going to come and drive me back to my flat in Clifden, isn't he? I might be able to get him to stay over, cos I'll need driving back here tomorrow morning. My car will still be here."

Lyons grinned an impish grin.

* * *

Next morning, Lyons got up at eight o'clock and made her way down to breakfast. She wasn't terribly hungry, so she settled for a poached egg on toast, and a pot of strong coffee. Stella was serving, and when she came to clear away Lyons' dirty plate, Lyons said to her, "Stella, I'd like to have a chat with you a bit later. When is a good time for you?"

She looked nervously at Lyons.

"When breakfast is over, I have a short break before we start cleaning the rooms. Say, around nine-thirty. Would that be OK?"

"Yes, fine. I'll come and get you."

Lyons found Stella easily at half past nine. She was just checking out a couple who had stayed the night at the hotel, and she was explaining to them how to get to Westport going via Letterfrack and Louisburgh.

"Thanks very much, Stella," the man said in a distinctly North American accent. As he collected his receipt, Lyons noticed him slipping a €10 note discreetly into her hand.

"Hi, Stella. Is there somewhere private we could have a word?"

"Yes. Let's go into the lounge. There'll be no one in there at this time."

Lyons followed her into the lounge, and they both took a seat at a round table near the window.

"Stella, I'm sure by now you've figured out that I'm with the police. I need you to tell me as much as you can about Aoife Gilpin."

"What do you want to know?"

"Everything. What did Aoife do here at the hotel?"

"Same as me. It's a small outfit. We all do whatever is required. Reception; waitressing; cleaning, you know," Stella said.

"Did Aoife have anything else going on here?" Lyons said.

"What do you mean?"

"Look, Stella, don't you want to help us find out who killed her?"

"I don't want to get involved. It's none of my business, and I'm not involved."

"Not involved in what, Stella?"

"I told you. I'm not getting into it."

"Listen, Stella, I don't want to have to take you in to the Garda station and make this official, but I need you to tell me what you know, and I need you to tell me now."

Stella fidgeted with her hands and looked down to the floor.

Lyons waited. She felt that Stella wanted to talk, but was scared.

"It could be me next. I'm scared," Stella said.

"Who are you scared of, Stella? What's going on? What was Aoife into?"

Stella's eyes welled up, but she met Lyons' stare.

"Aoife was bringing cigarettes into the hotel and selling them to the tourists. She told me there was good money in it, and wanted me to help her, but I refused. I didn't want to get involved."

"Where did Aoife get them, Stella?"

"I don't know. She brought them back from Galway after the weekend in her suitcase."

"How often did this happen?" Lyons asked.

"Every time she went to Galway. Most weekends."

"Did she sell a lot of them?"

"I think so. They were very cheap compared to the shops, so basically any smokers that came to the hotel bought them. Some of the locals bought them in the bar too."

"Did Mrs McMadden know anything about this, Stella?"

"I don't think so. Aoife was very careful. She often did the actual transaction outside at the back of the building. I don't think Mrs McMadden knew about it, but I could be wrong. She never said anything to us though."

"OK. Now, do you know if Aoife had a boyfriend, Stella?"

"I don't know, I don't think so. Why?"

"It's nothing. Well, thanks for what you've told me. I'll need you to drop into the Garda station here in Roundstone to make a statement of what you've told me. Ask for Garda Brosnan or Garda Fallon. OK?"

"Yes, OK. Do you think I am in danger?"

"I don't see why you would be. But if you see anything suspicious or anyone hanging around that you think shouldn't be here, give us a call. We're only just down the road in any case."

"OK. Thanks."

Chapter Twenty

When Lyons had finished with Stella, she went for a walk up along Fuchsia Lane. When she got to the place where Aoife Gilpin's body was found, she stopped and had a good look around. Often, in the past, Lyons found that revisiting the scene of a murder gave her some new morsel of evidence that proved to be the key to unlocking the case. But this time, no such revelation occurred. She spent more than half an hour just soaking up the place, but nothing came to her, and she found no new evidence anywhere.

On the way back to the hotel, she called Mick Hays, but the call went through to voicemail, so she left a brief message.

"Hi, Mick. Just to let you know I'm coming back to Galway this afternoon. There's nothing more I can do out here for now, and I need to get back to the city."

Back at the hotel, she went in search of Mrs McMadden, the owner. She found her in the kitchen overseeing the preparation of lunch. Lyons introduced herself discreetly, and the two of them went back into the lounge, where it was still very quiet.

"I know this has been a very difficult time for you, Mrs McMadden, and I won't keep you longer than necessary," Lyons said.

"Tell me about it. It's been truly awful. And that poor girl. Have you any idea who is responsible?"

"We are following a few different lines of enquiry, Mrs McMadden. But something has come to light that I need to ask you about. It seems that Aoife Gilpin was selling contraband cigarettes from the hotel. Did you know anything about that?"

Mrs McMadden looked appalled.

"That's absurd. We don't even sell cigarettes here, and all our rooms are no smoking too. You must have that wrong," Mrs McMadden said indignantly.

"Mrs McMadden, we have two separate witness statements confirming what I have said. There's no doubt. But are you telling me you knew nothing at all about it?"

"Of course I didn't. I still don't believe it, whatever your witnesses say. Who are they anyway?"

"I'm afraid I can't share that with you just now, Mrs McMadden."

"I thought not. You're making it up, aren't you?"

"I'm not in the habit of concocting stories, Mrs McMadden, especially in a case as serious as this. But if you tell me that this is all news to you, then I am obliged to believe you, however unlikely it may appear."

"Are you calling me a liar, Inspector?"

"No, Mrs McMadden, I'm not. But I have to say that I find it very surprising that this trade was going on here on your premises and you had no idea. What about your husband? Would he not have noticed what was happening?"

"Sure, he's hardly here. We don't see him from one end of the day to the other, and he's often home late as well."

"I see. Well at some stage we may need to talk to him in any case. Maybe you could ask him to call me when he gets a minute," Lyons said. She gave Mrs McMadden one of her business cards.

Before leaving the village, Lyons called to the Garda station to talk to Pascal Brosnan.

"Hi, Pascal. I'm sure Mary told you that she's gone into Galway on an errand for me. She should be back a bit later."

"Yes, she said. Inspector, I've been thinking. Do you really think Gerald Gilpin could be the father of Aoife's child?" Brosnan said.

"I couldn't say. But the DNA tests will tell us anyway. Did you stay over at Mary's last night?"

"Yes, otherwise I would have had to go back into Clifden this morning to collect her. I slept on the sofa."

* * *

On the way back to the city, Lyons called Mill Street. Sally Fahy answered the phone.

"Hi, Sally. I'm on my way back in. I should be there in about forty-five minutes. Look, can you contact Izzy O'Flaherty? I want her brought in for questioning, preferably by the time I get there. Don't be too heavy. No need to arrest her, just say we need to ask her a few questions."

"OK, no problem. But can I ask what this is all about, boss?" Fahy said.

"I felt when we spoke to her last time that she was holding back information. It turns out Aoife Gilpin was selling contraband fags up at the hotel, and she seems to have been getting them in Galway. So, I'm pretty certain Isobel knows more than she's letting on."

"I see. OK. I'll go and fetch her myself, and I won't let on what it's about till you get to talk to her."

"Great, thanks. Oh, and could you give Sinéad a call too and ask her when we are likely to have the DNA results Mary Fallon brought in earlier?"

"Yes, sure. See you in a while then."

* * *

When Lyons got to Mill Street, Izzy O'Flaherty was waiting for her in an interview room. Lyons wasted no time in getting to talk to her. She took Fahy with her too, in case they needed to roll out the old good cop, bad cop routine. In this case Sally Fahy would be the good cop. They took a seat opposite the woman, who was looking decidedly unsettled, and read out the usual mantra advising O'Flaherty of her rights.

"Why am I here?" O'Flaherty said.

"We just need to ask you a few questions about Aoife Gilpin, that's all," Sally Fahy said in a friendly manner.

"Do I need a solicitor?"

"That's up to you, Izzy, but you're not under arrest or anything, and you're free to leave at any time, so unless you feel it's absolutely necessary, it will just delay things."

O'Flaherty looked a little sour, but said nothing.

"I take it that's a 'no' then," Lyons said.

Izzy shook her head.

"Izzy, did Aoife ever mention a man called Anthony or Tony Miller to you?" Lyons asked.

"No."

"What about a man called Michael?"

"No."

"Did Aoife have a boyfriend here in Galway?"

"She did meet someone a few times, but I don't think it was serious. I saw him dropping her off at home one night. He had a flash car. But we never talked about him," Izzy O'Flaherty said.

"That's a bit strange. Surely she would have chatted to you about her date?" Lyons said.

"Well, she didn't. It's not my fault."

"How many times did you see this man, Izzy?" Fahy said.

"Once, maybe twice. I don't know!"

Lyons decided to change tack.

"You told us before that Aoife used to go shopping in Galway at the weekends. Did you ever go with her?"

"Sometimes."

"And what did she buy?" Fahy said.

"Clothes and things."

"What about cigarettes?" Lyons said.

"No. She didn't smoke. Neither of us do."

Lyons looked at her colleague, and nodded imperceptibly.

"Izzy, we have received information that Aoife was involved in the sale of contraband cigarettes in the hotel where she worked. We believe that she bought the cigarettes in Galway at the weekend, and then brought them out to the hotel a few cartons at a time. Do you know where she was getting them? Could this Anthony be involved?"

Izzy said nothing for quite a little while. She was obviously considering her options, wondering how much she should reveal about her friend's activities.

"I think I'd like that solicitor now please."

The two Gardaí looked at each other.

"Very well. It's your choice. But it will take a few hours to get him in, and you'll have to wait here in the meantime," Lyons said.

"But I need to get back to work. I could lose my job," O'Flaherty said.

"Izzy, you can't have it both ways. Now do you want a solicitor or not?" Fahy asked.

Izzy looked down at the floor and didn't speak for several minutes.

"No."

"So, just to be clear, you are declining the services of a solicitor. Is that right, Izzy?" Lyons said.

"Yes, I guess."

"Right. Now, I want you to tell me what you know about Aoife Gilpin and this illicit cigarette business."

Another long pause from the woman.

"She got them off a ship. There's a ship that comes into Galway harbour every Saturday. I think it collects scrap metal from one of the yards down there. She knows one of the crew, and that's where she got them. Am I in trouble?"

"Were you involved in this at all, Izzy?"

"No, no, not at all. I didn't want anything to do with it. It was her business."

"Was this Anthony bloke involved?" Lyons said.

"I don't know. Honestly. He might have been, but I'm not sure."

"Do you have a contact number for Anthony?"

"No, I told you, I didn't know anything about any of this."

"Did Aoife tell you the name of the ship?" Fahy said.

"No. But I think she may have mentioned that it was Polish, or something."

Lyons recognised that she was unlikely to get anything further from Izzy O'Flaherty.

"Right, Izzy, we may need to talk to you again, but you can go for now."

Lyons gathered up her papers, and the two Gardaí left the room. Izzy was shown out by a uniformed Garda.

Chapter Twenty-one

On the way back upstairs, Lyons asked Fahy to get on to Sinéad Loughran to expedite the results for the DNA that they had taken from Gerald Gilpin. She then went into her office and closed the door.

Lyons tried to call Mick Hays, but his phone was engaged, so she left a message with his assistant. While she was waiting for him to return the call, she looked up the number for the Galway Harbour Company. She got through almost immediately, and asked to speak to the duty manager.

"Ted Wilkinson, how can I help you?"

"Mr Wilkinson, this is Senior Inspector Maureen Lyons here from the Galway Detective Unit. I'm making enquiries about a vessel that comes into the harbour every week or fortnight, I think, possibly on a Saturday evening. It may be collecting scrap metal from one of the companies down along the quay there."

"Oh, yes, Inspector, that's the *Paola Marie*. What would you like to know?"

"Ah, right. Can you tell me where it comes from and goes to?"

"Hold on a second, I'll look it up for you."

Lyons could hear the noise of a keyboard and a few mouse clicks as Wilkinson consulted his system.

"It says here Kolo… Kolo… hang on a second, have you got a pen?"

"Yes, go ahead."

"K-O-L-O-B-R-Z-E-G, and before you ask, I have no idea how to pronounce it, I'm sorry. But it may make other stops on its way as well."

"That's OK. And what is the cargo listed as, Mr Wilkinson?"

"Let's see, it looks like general cargo, but I know that it takes scrap steel away," Wilkinson said.

"And how many crew would the *Paola Marie* have?"

"Hmm... usually eight, including the skipper. It says here the captain, a mate, a radio operator and four hands, oh, and a chef."

"Thanks. Any issues with the vessel?"

"No, none. She just comes and goes."

"And how long would she stay in port normally, Mr Wilkinson?"

"Just a few hours. However long it takes to load up. But I'm not here when this happens. It's usually on a Saturday evening."

"And would any of the crew go ashore while she was berthed?"

"Unlikely, I'd say. If the shops were open, the chef might go and get some provisions, but he probably doesn't speak any English, so I really doubt it."

"OK. Thanks very much, Mr Wilkinson. Just one more thing. Is she due in this weekend?"

"Hang on, I'll have a look."

He was back a moment later.

"Yes, depending on sea conditions, she'll be here about ten o'clock on Saturday. May I ask why the interest?"

"Oh, it's probably nothing. It just came up in connection with an enquiry I'm involved in, but it may not be important. Thanks for the information anyway, you've been very helpful."

"No problem, Inspector, glad to help."

Lyons ended the call and spent a few minutes processing the information Wilkinson had provided. Then her phone rang.

"Lyons."

"Hi. It's me. You were looking for me."

"Yes, thanks, Mick. Listen, have you got a few minutes?"

"Yes, sure. Pop up."

Lyons needed no second invitation. She went directly upstairs to Hays' office.

When she sat down with her partner, she told him what Izzy O'Flaherty had told them about Aoife's lucrative little sideline, and what she had discovered about the *Paola Marie*.

"I see. That puts a completely new slant on the whole thing. Any sign of the BMW driver?"

"No, not a vestige."

"So, what's your plan?"

"I don't have one yet. I was hoping you might be able to come up with something," Lyons said.

"OK. Well, we could of course get Customs and Excise to stake out the ship when it next appears, but I'd have to run that by Plunkett of course. He might think it was a bit of overkill for a few smuggled cigarettes," Hays said.

"Yes, but we don't know how extensive the scam is. They could be shifting millions of the damn things. Aoife Gilpin may not have been their only mark either. And I looked up the price of ciggies in Poland. Even if they were paying shop prices, there'd be a huge markup on them when they got here. It might be making them more than the scrap metal."

"I see what you mean. Look, let me have a word with the boss. I'm seeing him later anyway. I know the first thing he will ask me."

"Yes, so do I. Have we any evidence connecting the woman's death to the contraband, and the answer is no, we haven't. Or at least if we have, it's very tenuous."

"All right then. I'll bring it up at the meeting later. Will you be around for the rest of the day?"

"Yes, I will, though I'm a bit concerned about Sheila, so I might need to go out to see her later."

"OK. Well, let me get back to you then."

"Thanks. Are you OK?" she said, sensing that her partner wanted her to leave.

"Yes, sorry. Just busy."

Lyons got up and left him to it.

* * *

Back at her desk, Hays' words were bouncing around in Lyons' head. In order to get the resources that she needed, and to make her senior officers take her seriously, she needed to establish some connection between Aoife Gilpin's death and her little enterprise out at the hotel. She called Sally Fahy into her office.

"Hi, Sally, come in and sit down. Listen, Mick is trying to give us a hand with this cigarette smuggling thing, but he said that he would have a much better chance if we could establish some connection between Aoife Gilpin's death and the contraband."

"I think he's right, boss."

"He usually is, Sally. At least about police work. But don't ever tell him I said that. Have you heard anything back from Sinéad yet?"

"No, but she said she might have something by close of play today."

"OK. So, let's you and me go back over everything we have learned about the case so far. Can you get any paperwork and bring it in?"

"Yes, sure."

Lyons and Fahy spent nearly an hour going back over every aspect of the case, working quietly away in Lyons' office. Fahy held up a piece of paper and said, "Look at this, boss."

"What is it?" Lyons replied.

"It's Aoife Gilpin's account statement."

"What about it?"

"Well, it shows her money coming in from the hotel. But we were so busy looking at the other cash she was lodging, we may have missed the obvious."

"Don't keep me in suspense. What have you found?"

"It looks to me as if Aoife Gilpin was getting paid a lot less than minimum wage. She was only getting about €5 an hour, not even some weeks."

"So? It's not exactly The Ritz out there."

"No, I know. But it could mean something else, couldn't it? It could mean that Mrs McMadden is paying the girls a lot less than she should be because she knows they are making good money from selling tobacco," Fahy said.

"Hmm... I see what you mean. Do you think we should have another word with Mrs McMadden?" Lyons said.

"Yes, I do. But she's a tough old bird. You'd have to be to run that place through thick and thin. And it doesn't look as if her husband helps out a lot. It might be easier to try and break down Stella. I still think she knows more than she is letting on."

"Who do you think would have the best chance of getting her to open up a bit?" Lyons said.

"I'd go for the two out at Roundstone. What if we got Mary to meet her after work some evening, and arrange for Pascal to show up as well and put a bit of pressure on her?"

"Sounds like a plan. Do you want me to set it up?" Fahy said.

"Would you? I have to arrange to see my sister out in Athenry later on. See if they could do it sooner rather than later though."

"Yes, OK."

"Before you go, have we anything on this Anthony Miller?"

"Is that the guy in the BMW?"

"Yes, or maybe his name is Michael something or other, if you recall," Lyons said.

"Yes, I do. I'll ask Eamon if he has managed to find out anything about him."

"Thanks, Sally."

Chapter Twenty-two

After work, Lyons drove out to the farm that her sister Sheila and Séamus ran, close to Athenry. The traffic was light and she arrived soon after half past six. When she had parked up in front of the house, she got out and went around the back to the kitchen door.

"Hi, Sheila. Can I come in?"

"Hi, Maureen, of course. Gosh that was quick. I wasn't expecting you so soon. Have you eaten?"

"No, but I'm fine. I don't mean to barge in," Lyons said.

"Don't be daft. There's plenty, but Séamus won't be in for another hour, so I hope you're not too hungry."

"I'm fine, really, sis. I just wanted to see how things are going. Any news?"

"Hang on. I'll get you a glass of wine first. Is white OK?"

"Yes, perfect, thanks. Just the one though, I'm driving."

Sheila went off to get Lyons' drink, and when she came back they both sat at the kitchen table. The aroma of delicious cooking wafted through the air.

"So, what's the story?" Lyons said.

"Well, it's all good really. We had one of the local auctioneers out and he says the place is worth a good bit more than we thought. He reckons we could get over a million for most of the land, and still keep the house and a few acres around it. He said that sites along the road frontage would be worth around 100k each, and we could sell five or six of them subject to planning, of course. But he was sure that wouldn't be an issue. He's going to prepare a sales plan for us. But are you sure you're OK with it, Maureen?"

Lyons extended her hand and placed it over her sister's.

"Yes, of course. The important thing now is to make sure Séamus stays well. Nothing else matters. I know it will be a wrench for both of you, but these things do come along. It's not what happens to you in life that's important, it's how you deal with it. And you're doing fine."

"Thanks, Maureen. I needed to hear that. You're right. It will be a big change, but we'll make the best of it. Speaking of which, when is that hunky superintendent of yours going to make an honest woman of you?"

"Stop, will ye! Don't get me wrong, we've talked about it quite a bit, but we've taken the view that if it ain't broke," Lyons said.

"Yeah, I know, but if one of you popped your clogs there would be endless complications about inheritance and all that crap," Sheila said.

"I think Mick has all that sorted. Anyway, neither of us is going anywhere for a good few years yet," Lyons said smiling.

"I hope you're right."

Lyons and her sister sat chatting for another half an hour, then Sheila got up and saw to the meal. Séamus came in at half past seven looking a bit tired, but with rosy cheeks from the fresh air, and they sat down to a pleasant meal together. At soon after nine o'clock, Lyons made her excuses and left.

* * *

Back at home, Mick Hays was glad to see his partner had arrived back. He was watching the ten-o'clock news on TV, but turned it off when she came in.

"How are they all out in Athenry?" he said when Lyons had settled beside him on the sofa.

"They're in good form. And they have been told that the farm is worth more than they thought. So that's good news. Sheila was asking about us. She says if something happened to one of us, there would be a lot of nonsense to sort out about our properties and so on. But I told her you have it all taken care of."

"That's only partly correct, love. She's right. Obviously, our wills are in favour of one another, but there could be unpleasant tax issues to deal with as we're not actually married. The state hasn't adjusted to the idea of cohabiting couples living together as man and wife yet, or they have chosen not to as it probably provides a decent income stream to them."

"Can we do anything about it, Mick? That sounds nasty."

"We could always get married. That's if you'd have me," he said grinning. He put his arm around her shoulder.

"Oh, I don't know now. You'll have to form an orderly queue. But if that's supposed to be some kind of proposal, you have a bit of work to do on it yet." She leaned in and kissed him.

"Think about it. We could do a civil partnership thing if you don't want a big number," he said.

"Charming! A quickie at the registry office, I suppose." She gave him a dig in the ribs.

"I'll do whatever you want, Maureen. But Sheila is right. We probably do need to do something. Now, enough. Any more news on the Aoife Gilpin case?" Hays said.

"Oh, you old romantic you. I was hoping you'd have some news for me. Did you get to talk to Plunkett?" Lyons said.

"Yes, I did. He doesn't want a big dog and pony show down at the docks. He said if it turns out to be one impoverished sailor flogging a few cartons of cigarettes to feed his family back home, it could backfire on us very badly. And if we get C and E out in force with lots of blue lights and 4x4s it will attract the press and God knows who else."

"So, how do you think we should play it?"

"Low-key. I'll work up some kind of plan. Could I come down tomorrow morning and sit in on your briefing and see if we can pull something together?"

"Yes, of course, but try not to make it sound so biblical – 'Jesus came down from the mountain and sat amongst his disciples' kind of thing!"

Hays gave Maureen Lyons a playful slap.

"Wow, you're in some form. Tell you what. Let us both ascend upstairs and see if we can create heaven on earth."

"Now, Superintendent, that's what I call a plan," and she kissed him again.

* * *

The next day, Hays came to the morning briefing as promised. Lyons spoke first, explaining why Detective Superintendent Hays was in attendance.

"The Superintendent has a plan for how we can move this case along, based on the information that has come to light about the Polish ship. Over to you, sir," Lyons said. She was careful to respect her partner's seniority in front of her team.

"Good morning, everyone. OK, here's how I think we should move on this. We know the vessel will be arriving into Galway harbour on Saturday night at around ten. I'd like all of us to be down at the docks, but in plain clothes and unmarked cars. We'll have radios, but later today the inspector and I will go down there and do a reconnaissance on the place. We'll work out where best everyone should position themselves, and initially we will just observe. If it's OK with you, Maureen, I'll take overall control, and we can have uniformed officers and the Armed Response Unit on standby back here if things cut up rough. Any questions?"

"Would you like us to have sidearms, Superintendent?" Sally Fahy asked.

"Who is firearms-trained here?" Hays said.

Lyons, Fahy and Eamon Flynn all put their hands up.

"Yes, OK. If you get the paperwork organised, Sally, I'll sign it off. But it's vital that no word of this operation leaks out, so keep totally quiet about it. No idle chit-chat where you might be overheard. We'll have an operational briefing here on Saturday evening at seven o'clock. All right, folks?"

A murmur of assent went around the group.

When the meeting was over, Hays went back to his office and made a call.

"Hi, Liam, it's Mick Hays here from Mill Street," he said to the man at the other end of the call. "I wonder if I could trouble you for a small favour."

"Sure, no problem, Mick. What can we do for you?"

* * *

Lyons returned to her office to find a message on her answering machine from Sinéad Loughran. She returned the call.

"Hi, Sinéad, you were looking for me," she said when Loughran answered.

"Hi, Maureen. Yes, you sent in some DNA samples for us to compare with Aoife Gilpin's unborn child. I'm afraid there's no match with the sample you sent. Well, there is a little, but not enough of a match to show that the donor of the sample is the father."

"Sorry, Sinéad, are you saying that the DNA sample taken from Gerald Gilpin proves that he's not the father of Aoife's child?"

"Yes, that's exactly what I'm saying."

"And you're sure about it?" Lyons said.

"Yes, certain. I can explain the science to you if you like, but I've had Dr Dodd check it out too. We're positive."

"Right. Well thanks for trying. Oh, by the way, did you run the infant's DNA looking for a cross-match in our system?"

"Yes, of course. It's a very long shot that we would be able to identify the father that way, but we tried in any case. No luck there either, I'm afraid."

"Great! But thanks anyway, Sinéad."

"Hang on, there is something else. Aoife Gilpin's blood is Rh-negative, but the foetus is Rh-positive. And there's a fair chance that the father's blood type is group B too. So if you can find a man that knew Aoife with blood group B who is Rh-positive, then I'd be asking him a few questions."

"Cripes, Sinéad. What percentage of the male population is Rh-positive and group B?" Lyons said.

"I haven't a clue. But people with group B blood are in demand for donations, because you can't mix type B with A or O. And there's under twenty per cent of the population that are type B."

"Hmm... OK, so now you've given me an idea."

"There ya are then. Don't say I never give you anything! See ya!"

Lyons was always surprised at just how good-humoured Sinéad Loughran was, given the rather gruesome subjects she had to deal with.

Lyons called Sally Fahy into her office.

"Sally, this is going to sound weird, but humour me, will you?"

"Of course, boss. What's up?"

"Can you get onto the blood transfusion service here in town and get them to give you a list of donors with blood group B? Then see if anyone on the list has cropped up anywhere in connection with Aoife Gilpin's murder."

"OK, sure."
"Thanks."

Chapter Twenty-three

The team came together as arranged at seven o'clock on Saturday evening. As soon as everyone was seated, Hays addressed the group.

"OK, folks, here's the plan. What we're looking for is a transaction taking place between someone off the ship, the *Paola Marie*, and someone on the docks. Now, it's a bit tricky, because there are quite a few small roads in and around where the ship docks. Maureen, have you got the map of the area for us?" Hays said.

Lyons produced an enlarged map of Galway harbour and pinned it up on the board where they could all see it.

"The ship berths here," Hays said, pointing to an area adjacent to one of the large yards on the quayside.

"It has a crane on board that it uses to grab the scrap metal that's piled up near the quay wall, and load it into the hold. The crew will all be busy working the crane and making sure the load is properly distributed so the ship doesn't list when it sets out to sea again. But one of the crew, or maybe more, will come ashore with his consignment of cigarettes and meet someone on the dock to do the deal. I'd like us to be able to intercept this transaction if possible. But if not, we should at least be able to nab the buyer as he leaves the area."

"What are we going to do if we succeed in intercepting the sale, sir?" Eamon Flynn asked.

"Call in the troops. Get on the radio and summon the uniforms and the ARU who are standing by. With a bit of luck, they might get to impound the ship and all."

"Where should we take up position, boss?" Fahy asked.

"Right. Well, the inspector and I will be in O'Connaire's restaurant. I've arranged for us to have a window seat upstairs that will give us a good view of the harbour, so we'll see when the *Paola Marie* comes in. Then we'll radio everyone and get things going. Sally, I'd like you to park at Hynes Yard car park and await instructions. Eamon, can you drive into the harbour area and park somewhere convenient but not obvious – I'd like you to appear invisible, if that's not an oxymoron."

A subdued laugh went around the little group.

"Have you drawn firearms in case it gets rough?"

Sally Fahy and Maureen Lyons confirmed that they had.

"OK, then, let's get everyone into position by nine o'clock and do a radio check then. Inspector Niall Griffin is the co-ordinator here and he's on the radio too. He'll liaise with the ARU if needed. Niall has arranged for a couple of cars to position themselves at the level crossing down along the Lough Atalia Road before the Fairgreen Road intersection, in case our hero manages to get away down there. Just to confirm, everyone, our main objective is to lift the buyer with as much merchandise as we can get, and as a bonus, if we could grab the seller, all the better. I'd like to put a stop to this caper for once and for all," Hays said.

"Do we know if any of this is connected to Aoife Gilpin, sir?" Eamon Flynn asked.

"Not sure for now, but I'd say so. We'll know more later on if all goes well."

* * *

Hays and Lyons enjoyed a delicious meal in O'Connaire's restaurant overlooking Galway harbour as they prepared for the sortie later on. It was a cool, autumnal evening in Galway, with quite a breeze blowing in from the west. The sea inside the harbour wall was calm, but outside, in Galway Bay a few white tops were starting to appear on the waves.

"How do you think this will go, Mick?" Lyons said as she tucked into her dessert – a slice of lemon tart with fresh cream in abundance.

"I'm not sure. We're a bit light-handed, but Plunkett wouldn't go the whole hog for a few dodgy fags. But I've dealt with Polish criminals previously, as have you, if you recall, and if they decide to get rough, we could be in a spot of bother."

"Yes, I remember our trip to Poland when we were investigation the murder on the old bog road. But it wasn't all bad," Lyons said smiling.

"Easy tiger! I think if we are careful, we should be OK. But don't be afraid to use your weapon if you have to. How's Sally with a gun in her hand?"

"Fearless. Remember that jewellery heist in the centre of town a while back? She was amazing. No fear, just a determination to get the job done and minimise the danger to her fellow officers. She may well have saved my life."

"Good. But I'd still feel happier if we had a few more resources. Maybe I'll call down a jeep full of ARU lads just before we go in. I'll let on to Plunkett afterwards that I felt some of us were at risk. He can't argue with that."

"Good idea. Now, unless I'm much mistaken, there's our ship just coming around the corner outside the harbour," Lyons said, looking out the window and pointing with her fork.

"Yep! That's her. Eat up and let's go."

* * *

Once outside the restaurant, Hays used his radio to alert the others to the arrival of the *Paola Marie*. The vessel had slowed to a couple of knots as it manoeuvred slowly into position up against the quay wall. Eventually, one of the crew jumped down onto the quayside and tied off a rope that had been thrown to him from the deck on one of the bollards.

"Standby, everyone. Don't move in till I give the command."

He heard several silent clicks of acknowledgement on his handheld radio signalling that the team had understood.

The crane on board the *Paola Marie* started to work. It reached out from the ship towards the land, and dipped down to grab a mouthful of twisted, rusty iron which it retrieved onto the ship and dropped into the hold.

Before it had taken the second scoop, a dark-coloured BMW entered the harbour and drove around close to where the *Paola Marie* was anchored.

"We have contact," Hays said into his radio, "standby."

The car pulled up with its lights off, but Hays could still make out the shape of a male driver and a female passenger in the car. After a moment the man got out and stood on the jetty. Then another man carrying a large cardboard box came down the makeshift gangplank from the ship and carried it over to the BMW where it was placed in the boot. The driver of the car handed over something, and the crew member disappeared back up the gangway into the ship.

"Go, go, go," shouted Hays into the radio.

Sally Fahy and Eamon Flynn descended on the harbour in two different cars and intercepted the BMW as it sped towards the exit. The BMW tried a few evasive moves, but it was clear that unless he wanted to end up in the drink, the game was up. Fahy jumped out of the car and ran to the driver's door, while Flynn went to the other side.

Fahy had drawn her weapon, though the safety catch was still on, and pointed it at the driver.

"Get out of the car now, nice and easy. No sudden movements, this thing is loaded," she said. She held up her warrant card in her other hand.

The driver eased himself out of the vehicle with his hands raised.

"Turn around, hands on the roof," Fahy instructed gruffly, and the driver obeyed. She took his arms down one at a time and handcuffed the man before turning him around to face her.

"Name?" Fahy said.

The driver said nothing, but the woman who had been removed from the passenger's seat by Flynn in a similar manner shouted across.

"What's going on, Michael. I'm scared."

"Ah, Izzy O'Flaherty if I'm not mistaken. And who exactly is your companion this evening, Izzy?" Flynn said.

Izzy said nothing for a moment, but Flynn wasn't having any. He gave her a dig in the ribs with his weapon, and that seemed to loosen her tongue.

"Michael Miller," she said, sullenly.

Fahy read the two of them their rights, telling them that they had been arrested on suspicion of smuggling contraband tobacco. Fahy and Flynn put one each in the back of their respective cars, and then Flynn got on the radio.

"Flynn here. Two arrested in possession of contraband. We're taking them in to Mill Street now."

"Well done. What about the seafarer?" Hays said.

"He's gone back on board and pulled up the gangway. There's no way onto the ship from here now," Flynn said.

"Roger. Over and out."

Chapter Twenty-four

"C'mon, Maureen, we're not finished yet."

Hays took her hand and walked off in the direction of the slipway where the lifeboat station was, at the other side of the harbour. When they got there, Hays pointed to a rubber dinghy that had been left tied up at the foot of the slipway with two life jackets inside.

"What the fuck, Mick?"

"Fancy a little trip across the harbour?" Hays said to his partner, grinning broadly.

"Jesus! Are you serious?"

"Never more so. I got the lifeboat guys to leave this out for us. It's perfectly safe here inside the quay walls, and we'll approach from the seaward side, so no one will see us."

"Bloody hell. You're full of surprises," Lyons said.

They inched their way down along the edge of the slipway where the grip was better, and clambered aboard the little grey Avon dinghy. The lifeboat crew had left a completely silent electric outboard motor attached to the thing, and had told Hays it had about an hour's worth of power in. it. That would be plenty for what he had in mind.

Hays sat on the seat that was positioned near the aft end of the little boat, while Lyons sat on the gunwale near the front. Hays undid the painter securing it to a metal ring in the wall of the slipway, and started the motor which was indeed almost totally silent. He steered the dinghy out into the centre of the murky black water, and pointed it towards the *Paola Marie*.

As they approached the side of the larger ship, Hays put his finger up in front of his mouth signalling to Lyons to stay quiet. He inched the dinghy along the dark side of the ship, which seemed to Lyons to tower menacingly above them. As the dinghy bumped silently against the hull, a set of iron steps set into the side of the ship came into view. Hays indicated upwards with his thumb.

Lyons got the message, and although she was very uncomfortable with the idea, she started to climb up the ladder nervously. When she looked down, she could see that Hays had tied the painter of the dinghy to the lowest rung, and was coming up behind her.

Lyons climbed silently over the rail at the top of the boarding ladder, and ducked down low behind some rusty machinery on deck. A moment later, Hays was at her side.

"What now?" she whispered.

"We go below, and see if we can find the stash. I've called the ARU guys to come in close in case we need them."

They crept along the deck till they came to a companionway that was dimly lit by a couple of bulkhead lights, and started down steep steps. As they emerged into a small landing area, it was clear that they had found the crew's quarters. Hays moved silently along the narrow, panelled corridor, and looked into two of the rooms. They had bunks, and various personal items strewn around, but no sign of any cigarettes. There was a door at the end of the corridor facing Hays, and he approached it carefully, listening outside for any sound. He signalled to Lyons to come up close to join him, and when they were both together, he twisted the handle on the door, and launched himself inside, with his gun pointing straight in front of him.

The man inside the room, surrounded by stacks and stacks of Dorchester cigarettes, was very startled and let out a yelp. But it was clear that he had been caught red-handed, so having sized up his options very quickly, he raised his hands in surrender.

Hays tried his radio, but in the small confines of below decks onboard the *Paola Marie*, it simply didn't work.

"Name?" he said gruffly to the beleaguered crew member.

"Dawid," the man replied in a strong Polish accent.

"OK, Dawid, do you speak English?"

"Little," Dawid replied.

"How many crew are on board this ship, Dawid?" Hays said.

"Ten."

"Right, Maureen, can you go back up on deck and call in the cavalry? I'll keep Dawid company here till they are on their way."

"Right. Will you be OK?" she said.

"Yes, of course. Now go."

Lyons did as she was told. She retraced her steps back along the corridor, and at the end of it, she replaced her weapon in her holster attached to her belt, in order to climb up the steep stairway back onto the deck. But as she emerged, she was grabbed from behind in a vice-like grip, and wrestled to the ground. She couldn't see her assailant, but he pushed her roughly along the deck as far as the bridge of the ship where he opened the door and more or less threw her inside. He spoke roughly in Polish to another man who was seated in front of the ship's controls. Although he wasn't very well dressed, Lyons assumed him to be the captain.

"Well, what have we here? A stowaway, perhaps."

The captain nodded to his colleague, and the man found a piece of rope and tied Lyons' hands behind her back.

"I am Detective Inspector Maureen Lyons from the Galway police. We are seizing this vessel on the basis that it is being used for smuggling. Your ship is surrounded by armed officers on the quayside, Captain, so you'd better give yourselves up."

The captain smiled broadly.

"Very good, Inspector Maureen Lyons, but I'm afraid it's not going to be that easy."

The captain took up his own radio's microphone and barked some instructions into it. Lyons could see the crane retracting back on board, and being stowed. Two crew members ran out to the front of the vessel and started to undo the ropes that were mooring the ship to the harbour.

"What are you doing?"

"What we always do. We are setting sail for Poland. I hope you are a good swimmer, Inspector, because when we get, say, ten miles out, we'll put you overboard and you can swim home!"

"You'll be sorry, Captain. I have other colleagues on board, you know."

"Nice try, Inspector, but I'm afraid I just don't believe you."

* * *

Hays was wondering where Lyons had got to. He didn't want to risk moving Dawid on his own. The man knew the geography of the ship much better than he, and could spring any amount of surprises on Hays that might not end well. But he was becoming concerned that she hadn't returned.

He tried his radio again. Still nothing. He looked around the little storeroom, but couldn't see anything that would help him to secure his prisoner. Then he had an idea.

"Key," he said to Dawid.

The man initially pretended not to understand, but after a little prompting from Hays with his gun being used for encouragement, Dawid produced a key from a pocket in his overalls. Hays retreated, turning out the light in the storeroom. He backed out and closed and locked the door, leaving Dawid in the dark with his illicit cargo.

Hays moved quickly back along the corridor, and up the steps onto the deck. There was no sign of Maureen Lyons, or anyone else for that matter, so he made his way cautiously forward. When he reached the entrance to the bridge, he looked in carefully, and saw Lyons with her hands tied behind her back. He needed the element of surprise. He braced himself for what was to come, and as quickly as he could manage, he wrenched open the door to the bridge and jumped in screaming at the top of his voice, "Get down! Get down."

The captain of the ship reached underneath his desk, and started to pull out a weapon. But Hays was quick. He let off two rounds, one catching the man in the arm, and the other in the leg. Neither wound would be fatal, but they would hurt like hell, and require pretty immediate medical attention. The captain's gun rattled to the floor where Hays kicked it out of the way. The captain had fallen to the ground and was writhing in agony and moaning loudly. But there was another problem.

Before Hays had disabled the skipper, the man had put the ship underway, and it was moving slowly across the harbour towards the opposite quay wall. Crew members were running around in disarray, and the ARU officers who had been ready to board the vessel were standing hopelessly by, watching the drama unfold from the quayside.

Hays untied Lyons who promptly got on her radio and called, "Mayday, Mayday. *Paola Marie* adrift under power in Galway harbour. Urgent assistance requested. One wounded on board."

The crew member who had manhandled Lyons appeared at the door to the bridge, but when he saw the state of the captain of the ship, and Lyons standing there, now with her own gun on display, he ran to the side of the ship, climbed up on the railings, and jumped into the water. Lyons was quick to react.

"Mayday. Man overboard. He's in the harbour and he's wanted for questioning. Will somebody please rescue him and detain him, and any others who have the same idea."

Hays, who was a sailor himself, albeit on a pleasure yacht, sat in the captain's chair and brought the ship back under control. He positioned it back against the harbour wall where it had been to collect the scrap iron. The ARU officers had found a ladder from somewhere, and put it up to the side of the ship and had come aboard. They only took a few minutes to round up the rest of the crew and place them under arrest.

In response to the Mayday call that Lyons had put out, emergency services of all kinds had turned up along the quay, and paramedics came on board to see to the captain. He was taken away on a stretcher and loaded into the waiting ambulance.

Then Hays remembered Dawid. Both he and Lyons went below and released the man from his incarceration. He too was arrested and taken away to Mill Street for questioning.

When things had settled down, Hays and Lyons went back to the bridge of the *Paola Marie* and sat down.

"Christ, Mick, that was some shitshow," Lyons said.

"I know. Can you just imagine the paperwork!"

"What will happen to the crew?"

"I think they'll probably be released. Dawid won't though. I recognised him as the man doing the business with Miller on the quayside. He'll be done for illegal importation, tax avoidance, and a few other bits and pieces."

"And the ship?" Lyons said.

"Customs will seize it. It will probably end up as scrap. Ironic really. But you never know, once the politicians get involved, anything could happen."

"Hey. What about your rubber duck?" Lyons said.

"Oh, damn, yes, I'd forgotten about that in all the fuss. I'd better see if it's still there."

Hays went out on deck and peered over the side.

"Yep! Still tied to the ladder. I'd better go back down and take it back to the lifeboat station."

"Yes, OK. We'd better get back into Mill Street and see how Sally and Eamon are getting on with the other two anyway. I'll bring Miller's BMW in, and you can take our car."

"OK."

Chapter Twenty-five

It was after midnight when Lyons got back to the Garda station. Fahy and Flynn were still there.

"Hi, boss. God! That was some adventure. Are you OK?" Fahy said.

"Yeah, grand. I know it was a bit hairy there for a while, but we got a good result. Customs and Excise have seized the *Paola Marie*, and that guy Dawid will be spending quite a while as a guest of the government, I imagine. What about O'Flaherty and Miller?"

"We've bedded them down for the night in the cells. Neither of them said anything much. Izzy was pretty miserable though. I'm not sure to what extent she's really involved," Flynn said.

"Maybe. But she had been lying to us, so I don't think she's little miss innocent. But listen, folks, well done everyone tonight, and thanks for staying on. Let's get together at eleven tomorrow and we'll start to question our two friends downstairs."

"Did Superintendent Hays have anything to say about the whole thing, boss?" Fahy said.

"I left him boating around in the harbour in that dreadful little dinghy thing. I think he was glad that we both didn't end up being press-ganged and taken off to Poland. But he'll have a lot of paperwork to complete after he shot the captain of the vessel twice," Lyons said.

"Cripes! How did that happen?" Flynn said.

"The guy produced a weapon, and at the time I was tied up on the bridge."

"Do you think he would have shot you?" Flynn said.

"Yes, I do. He already had the ship underway. He could have sailed away and no one would have been any the wiser. Mick bagged up his weapon, so I imagine the skipper will have several charges to face, though, oddly, it's not illegal for the captain to have a gun on board, he's just not supposed to use it to shoot Gardaí. But that's for another day. For now, he's in hospital having a couple of bullets removed from his arm and leg."

* * *

Lyons got a lift home from one of the Gardaí on night duty. When she arrived, Hays was in the kitchen in his dressing gown. When they saw each other, they embraced warmly.

"God, Mick, that was a bit too close for comfort. Are you OK?"

"Yes, I'm fine. My clothes got a bit wet going back in the dinghy, hence my sartorial elegance. What about you?" Hays said.

"I'm grand. Glad that bit's over. You know I'm a landlubber. I hate those stupid little rubber boats," Lyons said.

"But you don't mind being tied up and whisked off to Eastern Europe by smuggling seafarers?" he said, grinning broadly.

"Well, I'd prefer a Caribbean cruise, but a girl has to take what she can get these days. Anyway, good shot, Mr Superintendent. The skipper won't be skipping around for a while now, will he?"

"It was lucky I kept my cool. I thought about a head shot – but oh, the paperwork!"

"On the subject of which, have you updated Plunkett?"

"Yes, I gave him a call when I got in. I'm not sure that he took it all in. He wants a full report in the morning."

"Typical. C'mon, let's go up. Tomorrow is going to be another long day."

* * *

Lyons was in bright and early the following day, as were the rest of the detectives. When she had procured a cup of nice strong, hot coffee, she gathered them together in the open plan.

"OK, folks. Busy day today. I want us to interview O'Flaherty and Miller as soon as. I don't want to give them too much time to put together some bullshit story that's half feasible. Eamon, can you go and see if they want solicitors and if so, do the necessary?"

"Yes, sure, boss. What about the Polish guy?"

"Let's leave him to stew for a while. He's banged to rights anyway, and I may let Customs deal with him. I doubt if he had anything to do with Aoife's killing. He would have been on the high seas at the time."

Flynn got up and left to do Lyons' bidding.

"Right, Sally, you and I will deal with the two suspects. Any preference?"

"I'd prefer Izzy, if that's OK?" Fahy said.

"Yes, fine. I'm looking forward to wiping the smile off that little shit's face anyway. OK. So, when Eamon gets back, let's get to it, and let's tic-tac after half an hour or so to compare notes."

Fahy asked Lyons about her adventures on the *Paola Marie*, and Lyons spent a few minutes telling the tale until Flynn returned to the office.

"Well, Eamon, what's the story?" Lyons said.

"Neither of them wants a lawyer. The bloke is cocky. Reckons he's done nothing and fancies himself as bloody

Perry Mason in any case. And Izzy is like a rabbit in the headlights, but she declined in any case."

"Excellent. Let's get on then. While we're busy downstairs, Eamon, can you follow up the other stuff on Aoife's blood group, and so on?"

"Oh, right, I'd forgotten about that in all the fuss," Flynn said.

* * *

Lyons entered the interview room where Miller was seated with his legs spread apart, lounging back against the somewhat uncomfortable chair that he had set back nearly three feet from the table, facing Lyons.

When she had recited the necessary for the recorder in the room, Lyons got started.

"Firstly, Mr Miller, can you confirm your full name and address please?"

"You know who I am."

"I need you to confirm your name and address please."

Miller looked away and sighed in an affected manner.

"Anthony Miller," he said, before providing his address, which Lyons noted was in one of the poorer parts of the city.

"Thank you. Can you tell me exactly what you were doing down by the harbour last night, Mr Miller?"

Miller suddenly sat upright, pulled his chair in close to the table, and leant in so that he was quite close to Lyons' face.

"You can call me Tony," he said in a half whisper.

Lyons pulled back a little from the man who was intentionally invading her space.

"Just answer the question please, Mr Miller."

"Nothing. I was just giving Izzy a lift."

"I see. And how do you know Ms O'Flaherty?"

"I met her before. I used to go out with that chick that got bumped off out in the sticks, and Izzy was her mate. When Aoife wasn't around anymore, we kinda got together. She's more fun than Aoife ever was, I can tell you that."

"So, what was Izzy's business down at the harbour late on a Saturday night?"

"I dunno. She just asked me to drive her. That's all I know."

"And did you not think it was odd when large cartons of what were quite clearly cigarettes were loaded into your car?"

Miller just shrugged, but said nothing.

Lyons remained silent for a few moments before continuing.

"Tell me about Aoife Gilpin, Mr Miller."

"What do you want to know?"

"How did you meet her? How long had you been seeing her?"

"I met her here in the city at that place, Hot Shots. I'm sure you know it," he said with a cheesy grin.

"How long ago?"

"I dunno. A few months back, I guess."

"And when did you become aware that Aoife Gilpin was involved in the contraband cigarette business?"

"I didn't. She never said."

"But you would have driven her to the docks a few times too, Mr Miller."

"No comment."

"So, are you telling me that the sum total of your involvement in this racket was driving Aoife and Izzy around while they collected thousands of cigarettes from that ship every week?"

"Yeah. I didn't even know what it was they were picking up. It just looked like a bit of a caper to me, so I went along with it."

"Who do you live with, Mr Miller?"

"Me mam. The dad died a few years back. It's just me and her at home now, and she's not very well."

"Of course, we'll be getting a search warrant for your house. I don't suppose that will go down too well with your poor sick mother."

Miller shrugged again.

"And we'll be requisitioning your bank account records too. Where do you work?"

"I work at a garage out on the Tuam Road. That big place with all the trucks outside. I'm a diesel fitter."

"Right. Oh, just one other thing. Where were you on the morning of 14 September, early doors?"

"I dunno. In bed, I imagine. Depends what time you're talking about. If it was a weekday, I get up at eight, and leave the house at twenty past to get to work for half-eight."

"OK, that's all for now. But I'll be back in a little while," Lyons said, getting up to leave.

"When do I get out of here?" Miller called after her.

She ignored the question and left the room.

Chapter Twenty-six

Lyons went back upstairs to her office and was joined a few minutes later by Sally Fahy.

"Hi, Sally. How did you get on with Izzy?"

"Not very well, I'm afraid. She says it's all down to Miller. She says he's the brains behind the whole smuggling thing, and herself and Aoife were just helping him out flogging a few of the ciggies here and there as a favour. Why? What does he say?"

"He blames the women, of course. Says he was just driving them around. Knew nothing about whatever they were up to."

"Bloody hell. Do you believe him?" Fahy said.

"Of course not. He's up to his neck in it. And he's a smart-arse to boot. I've a good mind to leave the whole mess to Customs to sort out, if it wasn't for Aoife's murder, that is," Lyons said.

"Do you think they had anything to do with it?"

"I don't know, Sally. I can't see a clear motive, or should I say, I can see several possibilities."

"Such as?"

"Jealousy. A row over the money. Loose tongues – maybe Aoife was blabbing about her little sideline and had to be silenced. But hang on, I have a plan."

* * *

Lyons went back downstairs, this time accompanied by Sally Fahy. They asked the custody sergeant to bring Dawid to the only other available interview room, which was known as the family suite, and was a bit more comfortable than the others.

"Well, Dawid, good morning," Lyons said as they took their seats on the rather basic, but quite comfortable sofa.

The Polish man looked dejected and worried.

"I need to get back to the ship," he said, with a slightly pleading look.

"We need to ask you some questions, Dawid. The sooner you answer them, the better it will be for you."

"OK."

"Dawid, how long have you been doing this business with the smuggled cigarettes?"

"You don't understand. My family will be in danger if I speak."

"How do you mean?" Fahy said.

"I am just a messenger, a sort of broker. I just pass out the merchandise and collect the money. There are others who arrange all of this, and they are very serious people. Now that we have been discovered, there will be a lot of trouble. My family could be killed."

"Is the captain of the ship involved in this business too?"

Dawid looked down at the floor but said nothing.

"Listen, Dawid. To be honest, I'm not that interested in your business with the tobacco. We have other people who deal with those things. But you see, one of the women that you have been selling these cigarettes to has been killed. And we need to know if there is a connection of some kind to her death."

"I don't know anything about that. All I do is carry the goods from the ship to the dock. Hand it over, and collect the money. Then, when we get back to Poland, two men meet the ship and I hand over the money. I get to keep a small amount for myself to feed my family. We are very poor, and I don't get much money for working on the boat," Dawid said.

"And do these men put more cigarettes on board?" Lyons said.

"No. That's another two men with a big van."

"And do you sell the stuff in every port you visit?" Fahy asked.

"Yes, of course."

"Tell me, Dawid, who pays you here in Galway, the man or the woman?"

"The man of course. I don't know why he brings those girls with him. He's stupid. They will talk to someone and get us all into trouble."

"So, that's Mr Miller, the guy who was driving the BMW?" Fahy said.

"Yes."

"Do you have any other contact with him ever?" Lyons said.

"I have a phone number for him so I can text if the ship is running late because of the weather, or something."

"We will need you to give us that phone, Dawid, and the phone number for Miller."

"OK. It's still on the ship, but you can have it if I can go now. I don't want the *Paola Marie* to sail without me."

"I shouldn't worry about that, Dawid. It will be here for a few days at least. Look, that's all for now. There are other people who will need to talk to you. Do you need anything?"

"No, just to get home."

* * *

When Lyons got back upstairs with Fahy, there was a message for her to call Mick Hays.

"OK, Sally. I'd better call the superintendent and see what he wants. Can you get hold of Miller's phone and check out what Dawid told us. Make sure it's preserved. Then go and charge Miller and hand him over to Customs and Excise."

"Right, boss. What about Izzy?"

"Let's hang on to her for a while. I want to ask her more about Aoife Gilpin later, but I better see what Mick wants."

Lyons retreated to her office and called Hays.

"Hi, Mick. What's up?"

"Guess."

"I don't know. I've been busy with that lot from last night. What's the story?"

"Plunkett has been bending my ear. He's had 'the call' from Dublin. The politicians are warming up to get involved, you know, 'Poland is a good friend of ours', 'we have a lot of Polish citizens here in Ireland doing good work', etcetera etcetera. And he's not too happy about me shooting the captain either."

"No, he probably would have preferred if the bloke had shot me instead," Lyons said rather crossly.

"I wouldn't go that far. But it complicates matters. How are you getting on with everything, anyway?"

"I'm still finding it difficult to make a link between the smuggling and Gilpin's murder. She was involved with the illegal tobacco scam, but I can't see how that would have got her killed. I'm going to have another go at her mate, Izzy O'Flaherty, later."

"And what about the Polish guy?"

"He says he's just a pawn in an extensive smuggling ring that's operating out of Poland. He just exchanges the stuff for cash and remits it when they get back to port and takes a small cut," Lyons said.

"Do you believe him?"

"Probably. Anyway, I don't care about that. I have a murder to solve, remember?"

"OK. Well, don't worry about the flak. I'll deal with that. I'll spin Plunkett some yarn that I haven't thought of yet and keep him off your back."

"Thanks, Mick. I'll keep you posted."

When she had finished the call, Eamon Flynn knocked on her door.

"Come in, Eamon. I hope you have some good news."

"Maybe, and maybe not. You know you asked me to check up on the blood donations for group B blood at the hospital?"

"Yes, what about it?" Lyons said.

"Well, you'll never guess whose name popped up as a donor for group B?"

"You're right, Eamon, I'll never guess, so just tell me, OK?"

"Sorry, yes, Liam McMadden, with an address at the Bertraghboy Bay Hotel, Roundstone."

"Wow! So, he could be the father of Aoife Gilpin's baby?" Lyons said.

"Possibly. Of course, he's not the only one that donates that blood, but he's the only one with any connection to our case."

"Thanks, Eamon, that's good work. See if you can find Sally for me and ask her to pop in, will you? I asked her to get some background checks done on the McMaddens a few days ago."

"Right, boss, will do."

It wasn't long before Sally Fahy appeared at Lyons' door.

"Hi, Sally, come in," Lyons said. She went on to explain what Eamon Flynn had told her about Liam McMadden.

"Cripes! I didn't see that one coming. What do you want to do?"

"Didn't you do some checking up on the McMaddens back at the start of all this?"

"Yes, I did. There's some stuff on my PC. Want to have a look?"

"Yes, definitely. Can you remember what he does for a living?"

"I think he's a builder of some kind, if I remember correctly. But let's check the system."

They went out to Sally Fahy's desk, and Fahy pulled up the information she had uncovered about Liam McMadden.

"Yes, here it is. He seems to specialise in refurbishing houses out across Connemara. Someone told us he does a lot of insulation work, reroofing, that sort of thing," Fahy said.

"Has he come to our attention previously?"

"No. There's nothing on PULSE in any case."

"OK. Well, look, I'd better get back out there and see if I can get to talk to him. Can you and Eamon manage here, Sally?"

"I guess. What about Izzy?"

"Why don't you both have a go at her. Put the squeeze on. I bet she knew about Aoife's condition, and she may even know who the father is. Do a really intense good cop, bad cop job on her. Tell her she's going down for her involvement in the smuggling – big it up a bit."

"I get the idea. Just one thing."

"What?"

"Can I be the bad cop?"

"Get outa here," Lyons said, smiling broadly.

Chapter Twenty-seven

It was mid-afternoon by the time Lyons set off on the well-worn path out along the N59 towards Roundstone. It was an overcast afternoon, but it didn't look like rain. When Lyons got clear of the city traffic, she called Roundstone Garda station, but the call was forwarded to Clifden as the station was, apparently, unoccupied. She got speaking to Séan Mulholland.

"Hi, Séan, it's Maureen. I was looking for Pascal or Mary over at Roundstone. Any idea where they are?"

"I do. There was a bit of a tip between two cars out on the old bog road near Murvey. Some Yank in a rented car forgot that we drive on the left. It's not unusual, but the car he hit was being driven by an old-timer who got a bit irate, so some onlookers called us. I sent Pascal and Mary out to smooth things over."

"Nobody hurt, then?"

"No. Only pride, and the rental car is a bit bent, I understand. Do you want me to get hold of them?"

"Yes, would you. I need them back at Roundstone. We have to see if we can find Liam McMadden. I need to talk to him."

Lyons went on to fill Mulholland in on what Eamon Flynn had discovered.

"Oh, I see. Mind you, we've never had any reason to talk to Liam McMadden ourselves, not that I can recall in any case. But I'll give Pascal a call and ask him to get back to the station. Let me know if you want me to do anything."

"Right, Séan, thanks."

Lyons drove on, and decided to leave it at that for now. She could have called the hotel and established where Liam McMadden was working, but she felt the element of surprise would serve her cause better.

* * *

Lyons pulled into the car park adjacent to Roundstone Garda station and was pleased to see the brightly coloured squad car was back outside. When she went in, both Mary Fallon and Pascal Brosnan were there nursing mugs of tea.

"Hello, Inspector," Fallon said, "can I get you a cup of tea?"

"Yes please, Mary, thanks."

Fallon went off to re-boil the kettle, making sure that the mug she would give Lyons was nice and clean.

When she had settled down, and taken a few sips of the hot liquid, Lyons asked, "Do either of you know where we could find Liam McMadden, the husband of Mrs McMadden from the hotel?"

"I think he's doing up a house over at Callow, on one of the narrow roads down to the sea opposite the island. It was an old, thatched cottage, but they got permission to extend it and replace the roof with a tiled one. He's been over there for a few weeks now with another couple of lads doing the place up."

"Excellent, Pascal. Do you think he'd be there now?" Lyons said.

"I don't see why not. Do you want to drive out that way and see if we can find him?" Brosnan said.

"Yes, that would be useful. I'll tell you more on the drive. Can we take the squad car? Mary, have you got a car here in case you have to go somewhere?"

"Yes, Inspector, I have my own car here if needed," Fallon said, "I have to see the American guy with the broken hire car anyway. He's staying in Roundstone tonight. The car rental company need a Garda report, it seems, though it's a whole lot of fuss over nothing, if you ask me. You can hardly see the damage."

"Great. So, whenever you're ready, Pascal, let's go."

As Lyons and Brosnan drove west along the N341 in the direction of Clifden, the sun began to peep through the broken clouds. It gave the ocean a deep aquamarine colour, which looked to Lyons every bit as scenic as the Pacific around the Caribbean islands. She explained to her colleague what had been discovered with the blood donations, and the results of analysis on the unborn child.

"Crikey, Inspector, does that mean that McMadden was the father?"

"We don't know. It's only a possibility at the moment, so we have to tread carefully. We can't just go barging in throwing accusations around without more evidence. What do you think yourself?"

"God, I don't know. Aoife Gilpin was a fine-looking woman, although she was very shy and reserved. I saw her a few times working the bar at the hotel if I went down there after work for a pint, or to listen to the music. I wouldn't have taken her for the type to get involved with him. He must be old enough to be her father."

"Yes, I know. But sometimes those quiet types can have lots of secrets. From what you say, I wouldn't have taken her for someone involved in smuggling either, but she definitely was."

"Here, I think this is the turn we're looking for. You can see scaffolding up all around the house further down the track," Brosnan said.

Lyons turned onto the narrow, single-lane track that led from the N341 coast road down to the sea. The ground all around was rugged and barren, with nothing but limestone rocks protruding from the stunted grass and reeds. But as they advanced towards the house, Lyons could immediately see the appeal of the place. The house had uninterrupted views of a small archipelago of several islands, dominated by Inishdawros, a large, almost flat, outcrop which in Irish is called Inis Dawhraí, or Oxen Island. At the end of the track was a small beach of pure white sand that would facilitate bathing in good weather.

"Nice place for a house. I presume it's going to be a holiday home?" Lyons said to Brosnan as they advanced on the property.

"Ah, most probably. Just another toy for some wealthy Galwegian or Dubliner to occupy for a few weeks in the high summer, I suppose."

"You're not in favour of all these holiday homes then, Pascal?"

"Ah, it's a mixed blessing, Inspector. Without them, there'd be nothing but ruins all across the landscape, and there'd be no one here at all, most likely. But they drive up the prices something shocking for the locals, and ensure that the young folks have to leave, or live with their parents till they're nearly old themselves, or until their folks die off."

"That sounds like the voice of experience, Pascal," Lyons said.

"It is. I'm the lucky one in our family that managed to find work here. I have two sisters that had to leave and go to the city when they had finished their schooling, and a brother who tried to make a go of it for a few years, but was eventually defeated by the weather and the poorness of the land. But that's another story," Brosnan said as Lyons pulled the car up in front of what would very soon be quite a spectacular dwelling.

When they got out of the car, they could see two men high up on the pitched roof nailing dark grey slates onto wooden battens that were strung between the rafters. Sheets of insulation flapped in the breeze, and there was no sound to be heard other than the tap tap of the hammers as they nailed the copper fixings into the roof. Brosnan called out to the men.

"Mr McMadden," he shouted up at them.

The older of the two men, dressed in working clothes and with a flat cap on his head, stopped hammering and looked down.

"Aye, I'm McMadden."

"I wonder if you could come down for a few minutes, Mr McMadden? We'd like to speak to you."

McMadden put down his hammer and clambered gingerly down along the bare roof trusses until he landed on the scaffolding board. He made his way to the ladders that were arranged in a zigzag shape, and descended to ground level. He walked over to the two Gardaí.

Brosnan introduced Lyons, and then himself and said, "Is there somewhere we could have a word, Mr McMadden?"

"We're grand here. Tommy can't hear us anyway what with the noise up there. What can I do for you?"

"Mr McMadden, am I right in saying that you are the husband of the lady that runs the Bertraghboy Hotel in Roundstone?" Lyons said.

"Yes, that's right. We own the place. Why? Has something happened?"

"No, no nothing like that, don't worry. Can you also confirm that you are blood group B and that you donate blood regularly at the Blood Transfusion Service at the University Hospital in Galway?" she said.

"Yes, that's right. I go in every three months, and they call me if they need me urgently. Why? What's all this about?" McMadden said.

"Mr McMadden, can I ask if you use polystyrene in your work at all?" Brosnan said, tuning into Lyons' interrogation methods.

"I do. In fact, I collect it from all around whenever I can. The bin men won't take it, so people have to get rid of it somehow, and it does me grand for insulation in roof spaces and between the cavities in walls. Why do you ask?"

"Did you collect any from Gerald Gilpin's place recently?"

McMadden stroked his chin, and then removed his cap to scratch his head.

"I think I did, but I can't be sure. But wait a minute. Yes, didn't he get a new TV there a few weeks ago and the thing was packed with that stuff. His daughter asked me if I wanted it one night when I was at the hotel, so I went up and got it the next day. I remember now."

"Did you know Aoife Gilpin well, Mr McMadden?" Brosnan asked.

"No, not well. I mean she worked at the hotel, so I'd meet her from time to time if I was home early and she was waiting tables or serving in the bar. It was a terrible thing that happened to her all the same. Mrs McMadden isn't the better of it yet. Have you found out who killed her?"

"No, we haven't, but we're following some definite leads. Can I ask you if you smoke, Mr McMadden?" Lyons said.

"Yes, I do. Not a lot, but if I'm having a drink, I usually light up."

"Do you have a packet of cigarettes with you now?" Lyons said.

"No, but there might be one in the truck. Why? Do you want one?"

Lyons nodded sideways at Brosnan who wandered off towards McMadden's pickup truck – a huge Ford number with a recent plate.

"How long more will you be working on this place?" Lyons said to fill in the time and keep McMadden focused.

"Yer man wants it watertight before the end of October, but we'll have to do the interior fit-out over the winter. He says he wants to be here from Easter next year, so there's no mad rush."

"Where's the owner from?"

"He's from Galway. He has a couple of coffee shops and a men's outfitters in the city centre. He must be doing all right out of it to be able to buy this place and have it done up like this," McMadden said.

"Have you seen the price of a cup of coffee lately? Scandalous!" Lyons said.

Brosnan rejoined the two of them, prompting Lyons to say, "Well we'd better let you get on with your work, Mr McMadden. Thanks for your time. We may need to talk to you again, but we'll try and give you a bit of notice next time."

"Ah, no bother. A bit of a break is always welcome. Good luck now." He turned and went back up the ladders to the roof to join his mate.

Back in the car, Lyons was first to speak.

"Well?"

"There's a pack of Dorchester wedged between the two front seats in yer man's truck."

"Interesting."

Chapter Twenty-eight

There was very little chat between the two officers as they drove back to Roundstone. They were both individually processing what Liam McMadden had told them, or more importantly, in Lyons' case at least, what he hadn't told them.

Lyons dropped Brosnan off at the Garda station at the edge of the village and continued on back to Mill Street. It was late in the day, but Flynn and Fahy were still at their desks.

"Hi, folks. Listen, sorry to ask you, but could you both stay on a while? I want to see if the superintendent is still here and have a chat about the Aoife Gilpin murder."

The two detectives reassured Lyons that there wasn't a problem, and she went off to find her partner. She was back a few minutes later with Hays in tow. The little group sat down in the open plan, and Lyons went through what they had discovered to date. They reviewed the entire business of the smuggled cigarettes, the place and manner of the killing of the young woman, and the events that appeared to be no more than a distraction, preventing them from getting to the heart of the matter.

"Right," Hays said, "here's what I think. There's a lot of ifs and maybes surrounding this case. Most of what you've uncovered is circumstantial, except for the smuggling. You need some hard evidence. Something that connects the victim into the story properly. Now, you could go straight after McMadden if you like, but he'll probably deny everything, and you'll have a hell of a job to prove his connection. I doubt if he'd willingly agree to a DNA test. He has too much to lose."

"So where does that leave us?" Sally Fahy asked.

"The more I think about it, the more I believe that the whole contraband cigarette thing is just a sideshow. Obviously, there's some connection, but I don't think it's why she lost her life. I think the answer lies in Roundstone, and more specifically at the Bertraghboy Bay Hotel," Hays said.

Lyons was anxious not to allow Hays to completely take over her case, so she cut in.

"So, why doesn't Sally go out there tomorrow and give that girl Stella a good rattle? She must know something about what's going on. And I think if you put her under pressure, she might just come across with what's really been happening. Are you up for it, Sally?"

"Yes, of course. I'll go direct from home and get there while breakfast is still being served, so I can make sure Stella is around."

"Great. I'll call Pascal when we're finished here and put him in the picture. And I want you to let me know as soon as possible if you get any useful information. I want to move quickly on this now, if we can. It's been going on long enough."

* * *

It was a grey, wintery day when Sally Fahy set off for Roundstone. It was raining hard, and the wind was up, lashing the rain against the car windows as she drove out along the N59. Winter was definitely approaching. Things weren't any better out west. The stiff breeze was blowing the rain almost horizontally across the road from the sea side, and Fahy had to stay alert to make sure that she didn't get blown off course by the wind.

Fahy parked as close as she could to the hotel's front door and got out, wrapping her raincoat tightly around her. She made a dash for the door, but had to stand back at the entrance to allow a couple towing a large black suitcase behind them to come out, making slower progress than Fahy would have liked. Eventually, she managed to get inside, her hair blown all across her face and the front of her mackintosh stained dark with rain. She made for the toilets, where she managed to restore some semblance of a respectable appearance, and then went into the dining room.

She took a seat by the window, noting that there were still a few couples finishing their early morning meal. The smell of frying food and coffee pervaded the air, and she realised that she was in fact quite hungry. After she had settled down, Stella appeared with her order pad and pencil in hand. She was dressed in the standard uniform for a waitress – black pants and a crisp white blouse.

"Oh, hello again," the young woman said, "I didn't realise you were staying here."

"I'm not, Stella. I drove out this morning. Listen, after I've eaten, could we go somewhere and have a little chat?"

"Yes, of course. What can I get you for breakfast?"

Fahy ordered a poached egg, toast and coffee and Stella went off back into the kitchen to see to the order, returning a few moments later with a pot of coffee and the usual accessories.

"Your breakfast will be along in a minute," she said, placing the coffee pot down carefully on the white tablecloth and turning Fahy's cup upright.

"Thanks, Stella. Is the hotel busy at the moment?"

"We had six couples in overnight, but it's definitely thinning out now. In another couple of weeks, we'll be lucky to have anyone at all."

Fahy's breakfast appeared a few minutes later. It was well cooked and nicely presented, and she enjoyed what was on offer. When she had finished, and Stella came to clear away, Fahy said, "Where could we go for our chat, Stella?"

"Give me five minutes and meet me in the lounge. There'll be no one in there at this time. OK?"

"Yes, fine thanks."

Fahy took a seat in the lounge and looked out at the unrelenting deluge battering the window.

"Cripes, it sure knows how to rain out here," she said to herself.

Stella arrived a few minutes later and sat opposite Fahy at a small round table that had frankly seen better days.

"What did you want to talk to me about, Sergeant?" Stella said.

"It's about Aoife Gilpin, Stella. I want you to tell me all you know about her."

Stella shifted uneasily in her seat and avoided eye contact.

"There's not much to tell. You know just about everything about her now, don't you?"

"No, Stella, we don't. Did you know that she was pregnant?"

Stella said nothing.

"I take it that's a 'yes' then. When did you find out?"

"She told me the week before she was killed. She'd done a test herself, but she had been to a doctor in the city, and he confirmed it."

"Did anyone else know?" Fahy said.

"No, no, definitely not. She was scared stiff about what her parents would say. Especially her dad. Aoife was daddy's little girl, and could do no wrong. She said he'd probably throw her out."

"What was she going to do?"

"She didn't know. But she had been trying to research abortion, I know that. But she said she'd have to go to England so that her parents didn't find out, and she didn't know how she was going to get there, or anything."

"Stella, do you know who the father was?"

Stella looked away again, but this time remained silent.

"It's important we establish his identity, Stella. Remember, your friend was killed in a most brutal fashion. For her sake, you need to tell me all that you know."

"She said she only went with him twice, and she couldn't understand how she had got caught," Stella said.

"Tell me about it, Stella."

"It was in the summer. The hotel was mad busy, and Aoife would sometimes stay over in one of the guest rooms if the music went on late and she had to clear up. She told me one night after everyone had gone, Mr McMadden was hanging around and gave her a couple of drinks. Next thing she knew they were kissing, and he took her upstairs. She didn't remember much after that, but she said they had 'done it'."

"I see. And did this happen more than once?"

"Yes, I think so. Maybe a few times."

"So, Liam McMadden is the father of her baby?"

"Yes, I guess so. She didn't sleep with anyone else. She wasn't the type."

"What about Anthony Miller? The guy with the flash car."

"Oh, no, definitely not. That was just business."

"I know this is hard, Stella, but did Liam McMadden ever come on to you?"

Stella flushed visibly.

"Yes, he did. Same thing. Late one night when the place had been jumping, and I was staying back to clear up. He came over all friendly, and poured me a huge vodka and tonic. But I rejected him. Told him to lay off, or I'd tell Mrs McMadden. He got the message."

"And where was Mrs McMadden when all this was going on?" Fahy asked.

"She usually went to bed at about half-ten or eleven. She's up very early every day to see to the breakfasts, and she gets tired, so she goes up around that time."

"Do the McMaddens sleep here?"

"Yes. They have nice quarters down the back of the new wing. It's quite private and very nicely done out."

"OK, Stella, thanks for being so honest with me. I'll have to ask you to come into the station to make a statement in a few days. Just one other thing. What time does Mr McMadden usually leave in the mornings to go to work?"

"It varies, depending on how busy he is. But he's been working hard lately, so he's been leaving soon after eight."

"One last question, Stella. Was Aoife Gilpin happy working here?"

"No. Not after what happened. I think she was planning to go to England to get, you know, and then not come back. That's why she was saving up so much."

"Great, thanks again."

Chapter Twenty-nine

"Hi, boss, it's me. I've finished interviewing Stella out here at the hotel. She believes that Liam McMadden may be the father of Aoife Gilpin's child. By the sounds of it, it seems he got Aoife tipsy and then took advantage late one night after hours."

"I see. I must say, I had my suspicions. I didn't take to the man," Lyons said.

"What do you want me to do now, boss? Do you want me to take Pascal out and pick him up?" Fahy said.

"No, not yet. After all, sleeping with a woman of twenty-three and getting her pregnant isn't actually a crime. It's pretty reprehensible, but not actually illegal."

"Yes, but that gives him a strong motive for bumping her off, doesn't it?" Fahy said.

"That's a leap we are not entitled to make just yet, Sally. We need some evidence to tie him to the crime, if indeed it was him at all. You'd better come back in for now. I'll see what I can do from here," Lyons said.

"OK, if you're sure."

"Yes please, just come back to the station."

* * *

Lyons was busy preparing the paperwork from their adventures aboard the *Paola Marie*, and didn't notice the time slipping by. Customs and Excise had advised her that they had seized almost four million euro's worth of contraband cigarettes on the vessel, so it didn't matter what sort of fuss the politicians made, there would be prosecutions and seizures for all the crew and the ship itself. It was late afternoon when she looked up from her desk and saw the time.

"Shit! I'd better get the troops together. I didn't realise it was so late," she said to herself, as her stomach growled for lack of food.

When they had gathered in the open plan, Lyons began.

"OK, well by now you will have heard the latest from Roundstone. I need us all to focus on how we can find out for sure if Liam McMadden had anything to do with the murder of Aoife Gilpin. There's a good bit of circumstantial, but nothing concrete, and the way things are going, he's the only promising lead we've got. Tomorrow, I want you all to focus in on this and see if we can come up with anything useful. Eamon, will you call Séan Mulholland and see if he has any ideas? Sally, I want you to go back over every scrap of evidence again to see if we've missed something, no matter how small. I'm afraid I'll still be tied up with the smuggling thing for most of the day, but call me if we discover anything useful."

Just as they were about to break up and go their separate ways for the night, the phone rang. Lyons picked it up.

"Lyons."

"Hi, Maureen. It's Sinéad. Listen, I'm really sorry about this, but I've found something that we missed earlier. I was having a look at those black plastic sacks that were brought in from Roundstone. You know, the ones that were placed across the road to stop Aoife Gilpin in her tracks."

"Yes, and…?"

"Well, I turned them inside out for some reason, and stuck to the inside down at the bottom of one of the bags was a petrol receipt. It's for diesel, and it's date and time stamped. It must be quite a big vehicle, cos the receipt is for €200."

"Cool. Where was it issued?"

"Looks like the Topaz petrol station in Clifden, and it was printed two days before Aoife was murdered."

"OK, thanks, Sinéad. Could you scan it and email it to me quick as you like? I'll get someone working on it as soon as I get it," Lyons said.

"Sure, and I'm sorry we missed it earlier," Loughran said.

"Not to worry. Glad you found it though. It could be helpful."

Lyons told the rest of the group what Sinéad Loughran had told her.

"When this comes through, Eamon, can you get on to Séan Mulholland. Ask him to send someone down to the Topaz station in Clifden and see if they have CCTV for the time that the receipt was issued. Let's see if we can identify who bought two hundred euros' worth of diesel."

"Right, boss."

* * *

"Hello, Séan. It's Inspector Flynn here from Mill Street. Listen I need you to do something for me. Could you send someone down to the Topaz petrol station there, and ask them if they have CCTV for the 12 September at nine-thirteen the morning. If they have, collect it and get someone to drop it into us here. Is that OK?"

"Hello, Inspector. Yes, we can do that. Will it do in the morning? Jim is off out with the car at the minute."

"It would be better if you could manage it this evening, Séan. It could be the key to unlocking the Aoife Gilpin murder case," Flynn said.

"Oh, right, so. I'll go down myself when I've finished my cup of tea and see what we can find," Mulholland said.

"Thanks, Séan. Maybe you could give me a call back if they have it still?"

"Very well, Eamon, will do."

Mulholland wasn't best pleased. He'd have been OK with it if Maureen Lyons had asked him. Somehow, he seemed to get along really well with her. But for some reason, he wasn't that keen on Flynn, although, in fairness the man had never caused him any bother. When he had finished his mug of tea, he put on his cap, and set off down the road towards the Topaz station which was located just a few hundred metres from Clifden's Garda station.

* * *

"Hi, Mick, it's me. Are you nearly finished for the day?" Lyons said.

"I could be. Why?"

"I'm bloody starving. I completely forgot about lunch, and I need food, alcohol, and good company in that order. You up for it?"

"Give me five and I'll see you downstairs. Sounds urgent."

"It is. See you."

They didn't want to go too far to get Lyons the sustenance she needed, so they walked briskly around to An Béal Bocht and got a nice quiet table near the back of the little bistro. The place wasn't too busy as it was only just half past five, and they were attended to by the ever-pleasant maître d' almost at once.

"This woman needs one of your best sirloin steaks with all the trimmings, medium rare. And I'll have the same, along with a bottle of your finest chardonnay, Peter."

"Coming right up, folks. Some bread and olives to start?"

"Perfect," they said in unison.

Moments later Peter delivered a small bowl of green pitted olives, some fresh ciabatta, and a little saucer of extra virgin olive oil.

"So, what's the craic?" Lyons said, dipping a slice of the bread in the oil.

"I had a call from your brother-in-law earlier. He was looking for a bit of advice about the farm. Turns out the farmer that has the adjoining land is interested, and he was asking if I knew anyone that could act as honest broker between them."

"Wow, that didn't take long. Were you able to help?"

"I told him I'd be useless in that capacity, but the truth is, I just don't have the time. But I said I knew someone who might be able to do it, but that there would be a fee involved. He said that was fine. So, I gave our old friend James McMahon a call, and when James heard the full story about Séamus, he said he'd be delighted to help. He's pretty sound, is James, despite his liking for pretty Eastern European girls."

"Ah, that's helpful, Mick. Thanks. It's important that they get a decent price for the place, and James will look after his interests. Will it cost Séamus much?"

"That's between the two of them, but I'd say James probably won't charge him anything at all. He likes to keep in with us," Hays said.

"And that won't cause you or me any issue with GSOC or anyone later on, I hope?"

"It shouldn't. But if it all works out, I'll get James to issue a fee note and I'll pay it, to keep things squeaky clean."

"Thanks, Mick. You're a good man," Lyons said. She put her hand over his on the table and squeezed it gently.

Their meal arrived, and they tucked in hungrily till there wasn't a morsel left on either plate. Peter came back and tried to get them to take a dessert, but they were both full, so they declined and just sat chatting for a while.

"Now what was that about wanting good company, Inspector Lyons?" Hays said with a glint in his eye.

"Yes. I know just what we need for dessert, but not here," she said smiling, and the two left to go home to their love nest in Salthill.

Chapter Thirty

At just after half past one in the morning, Pascal Brosnan's mobile phone began to chirp on the nightstand beside his bed. He was in a deep sleep, and couldn't understand at first why his alarm was going off in the pitch dark. Shaking himself out of his slumber, he reluctantly picked up the device and pressed the green answer button.

"Is that Garda Brosnan?" said the voice of a clearly distressed woman at the other end of the call.

"Yes. Who's this?" he said.

"It's Eileen McMadden up at the hotel. Sorry to ring you so late, Guard, but I'm worried about Liam. He hasn't come home, and it's not like him at all."

"I see. When did you last hear from him, Mrs McMadden?"

"This morning. We had breakfast together at around seven-thirty, and then he went off to work. He's in a hurry to finish the roof on that place out at Callow before the winter sets in."

"And what time were you expecting him back, Mrs McMadden?"

"He never works on after the light goes. It's too dangerous. So he should have been back here at about half past eight."

"Maybe he just went for a few drinks with his mates and is staying with one of them. Have you tried to call his mobile?"

"Yes, of course. But it just goes through to voicemail. I'm worried sick."

"Perhaps his truck broke down, and he's had to walk somewhere for help or something," Brosnan said, struggling to find excuses for why the man might not have gone home.

"That's nonsense. Sure, isn't only a new thing he has. No. There's something wrong, Guard. Can you do something?"

"Not at this time of night, Mrs McMadden. There's no point going out looking for him in the dark, he could be anywhere. And he's not been missing very long now, has he?"

"It's just I have a bad feeling, Guard. When can you start a search?"

"Officially, not till he's been gone for forty-eight hours. But I can have a drive around myself in the morning, and ask the lads from Clifden to keep an eye out."

"God! Is that the best you can do?"

"I'm afraid so, Mrs McMadden. But try not to worry. These things almost always resolve themselves quite quickly. You'll find that there's a reasonable explanation tomorrow, and you'll kick yourself for being so distressed. Trust me. I've seen this many times before."

"Hmph. That's easy for you to say. I'll not sleep a wink for the rest of the night. What time will you start looking in the morning?"

Brosnan was getting a bit fed up with the woman's persistence.

"As soon as I can, Mrs McMadden, now don't worry."

Brosnan ended the call at that, turned over, and went back into a deep sleep within minutes.

* * *

Lyons arrived at Mill Street at eight o'clock the next day to find an envelope waiting for her at the front desk. She opened it as she climbed the stairs to her office, and found a DVD inside in a clear plastic sleeve with a handwritten note from Séan Mulholland.

'CCTV from Topaz for the time you requested, Séan,' was written in the man's unique handwriting style on a compliments slip. When she got upstairs, she called Eamon Flynn and Sally Fahy over to one of the office PCs that had a DVD drive attached. Fahy clicked the mouse a few times and pressed a few keys on the keyboard, and a moment later an image of the garage forecourt filled the screen. There was a time stamp going along the bottom of the image as vehicles came and went filling up with fuel. At eight minutes past nine in the morning a newish Ford pickup truck pulled up to the diesel pump, and Liam McMadden got out. He spent a few minutes filling the truck with fuel, replaced the nozzle and went into the shop to pay. He was seen coming back out at nine-fifteen according to the time shown on the video.

"Gotcha!" said Lyons. "Well done, Sinéad! So that connects Liam McMadden to the bags that were put across the road to block Aoife Gilpin as she cycled to work on Fuchsia Lane. Fantastic. I think we need to pay Mr McMadden another visit. I'll give Pascal Brosnan a call and set it up."

Lyons went off to her own office, having instructed Eamon Flynn to enter the DVD into evidence, along with the scan of the receipt from Topaz.

She called Roundstone. The call was answered by Mary Fallon.

"Hi, Mary. Is Pascal there, please?"

"Eh, no, not yet, Inspector. He had a call during the night and is running a bit late. He'll be here in a few minutes. Can I help at all?"

"It's fine, Mary. Just ask him to call me when he gets in, will you?"

"Yes, of course."

While Lyons was waiting for Brosnan to call, she took a large sheet of paper and drew out one of her famous spider diagrams. She put Aoife Gilpin at the centre in a circle, and drew lines out from it. 'Tobacco Smuggling'; 'Pregnant'; 'Izzy O'Flaherty'; 'Anthony Miller'; 'Dawid'; '*Paola Marie*'; 'Gerald Gilpin'; 'Stella', and the 'Bertraghboy Bay Hotel' all appeared surrounding the central circle, with lines going out from Aoife Gilpin's name to the others. She spent a few minutes staring at the diagram, and then it all began to make sense to her. Her thoughts were interrupted by her phone jangling on the desk.

"Lyons."

"Hello, Inspector. It's Pascal Brosnan. You were looking for me."

"Hi, Pascal. I hear you had a busy night."

"Ah, all nonsense. That woman from the hotel was on saying her husband hadn't turned up. He probably had a few drinks in Clifden after work and got lucky, but of course I didn't suggest that to the missus."

"OK. Well, that's why I wanted to speak to you. We need to go out to Callow again and speak to the man. Something has turned up."

"Oh, right. Do you want me to head out there now?"

"No. Wait till I get there. I'll have Sergeant Fahy with me, and we'll be bringing Mary Fallon too. OK?"

"Oh, right. When will you be here?"

"In about an hour. Can you phone Séan Mulholland and just let him know what's going on?" Lyons said.

"Yes, of course, See you soon."

On the way out in the car, Lyons explained to Fahy what she had figured out from the diagram she had drawn in her office.

"There's something missing though, isn't there?" Fahy said.

"Well spotted, Sally. We'll make a detective of you yet!"

"Gee, thanks!" Fahy said, chuckling. "She was blackmailing him, wasn't she?"

"That's my guess. I doubt if he would have killed her just because she was pregnant. There had to be more to it, and Stella told you that Aoife was saving like crazy to get away. When we get to talk to him, we should be able to clear that up. It might go a little towards mitigation when it comes to court," Lyons said.

"Jesus! The messes that some people create for themselves. Honestly!" Fahy said.

"I know, and we usually have to try and disentangle the whole crazy business and get to the bottom of things. Still, it's what we do."

They arrived at Roundstone Garda station a short while later. The day was overcast, but at least it wasn't raining. Not yet, in any case. Inside, Pascal and Mary were ready for the road.

"What cars do you want us to take, Inspector?" Fallon asked.

"I want you and Pascal in the squad car. Sally and I will stick with mine, but you two go first," Lyons said.

"Lights and sirens?" Brosnan said.

"No, I don't think so. Unless he tries to make a run for it, then all bets are off. But I don't think he will."

They drove out in convoy along the N341 until they were abeam Inishdawros Island, when they turned down towards the sea and the house that McMadden was doing up. As they approached, they saw that his truck was there, but there was no sign of the man on the roof, nor any of the second man who had been helping on the previous occasion.

"See. I told his wife not to be worried," Brosnan said to his companion.

They pulled up adjacent to McMadden's truck, and got out. There was no sound to be heard other than the occasional noise of a curlew off in the distance. There was no sawing, no hammering, no radio playing; in fact the place was eerily quiet.

"You two stay here by the truck in case he makes a run for it. Pascal, you and I will go in."

They picked their way over some planks of wood and other building materials that had been discarded in front of the house, and stepped inside the opening where the front door had yet to be fitted. Inside, there were block walls erected to divide up the space, but in what would become the hallway, a vaulted ceiling was left to take full advantage of the steeply pitched roof. Bare rafters stretched up to the apex, with beams going across at equal intervals, and there, hanging by rope from one of the beams, was the limp form of Liam McMadden.

"Bloody hell! Can you get a ladder or something, Pascal? We need to see if by any chance he's still with us."

Brosnan went back outside and took one of the aluminium ladders that was part of the scaffolding arrangement and brought it inside. Fahy and Fallon asked him what was going on, but he didn't reply. He just told them to stay outside and continued with his mission to get up to the unfortunate man to see if he could perhaps save him. But it was to no avail. McMadden's body was hard, stiff and cold. Rigor mortis had set in.

"It's no use, boss. He's been gone a while. Do you want me to cut him down?" Brosnan said from his perch high up in the roof space.

"No, Pascal. Leave him be. We'll get an ambulance and the fire service out and let them look after him. Give Séan a call and ask him to get things moving."

Brosnan came back down the ladder and made the call.

Lyons called Sinéad Loughran and told her what they had found.

"Can you get Dodd out? He needs to certify death and have a look to make sure it's suicide, but I don't think there's any doubt."

"Yes, poor man, of course. Is there anything else I can do, Maureen?"

"No, not for now in any case. Thanks, Sinéad."

Lyons walked over to her two female colleagues.

"Is this your first, Mary?"

"Yes, boss. I'm afraid so."

"Well, at least it was quick, and no gratuitous violence. The rope snaps the neck immediately. They only last a couple of seconds usually."

"What are we going to do now, boss?" Fallon asked.

"I'd better wait here till the circus gets here. I'd like to see if there's a suicide note. If you two want to get off and go and tell his wife, that might be best. We don't want her finding out from anyone else."

"OK," Fahy said. "Will you give Pascal a lift back later?"

"Yes, of course."

Chapter Thirty-one

Lyons waited at Callow until the fire brigade and ambulance arrived out from Clifden. While she waited, she strolled down to the end of the lane and sat on a rock overlooking the small, white sandy beach and the islands offshore. She wondered how such terrible tragedy could occur in such a truly beautiful place, and if somehow, it would impact on the beauty that surrounded her. But then she remembered that the place had seen sadness before during the famine years in the mid 1800s, and had apparently recovered.

When McMadden had been carefully lowered to the ground by the firemen, and laid out on his back on the floor, Lyons returned. She donned blue vinyl gloves and gently probed the pockets of Liam McMadden's blue jeans, where she found a note folded over and tucked away.

> *Dear Eileen. I am so sorry. I have done some terrible things, and I hope this will draw a line under them. I didn't mean to kill the girl, but she was blackmailing me, and I knew that it would just go on getting worse till I couldn't afford it anymore, and I couldn't stand the shame that would be brought on us both, and you*

in particular. I know they say that this is the coward's way out, but I feel I have no choice. You know I always loved you. Liam x

Lyons placed the pathetic note into an evidence bag and tucked it away in her inside jacket pocket. She was in no hurry to share it with anyone, though she knew, by rights, she should give it to the man's wife. Just not yet.

Dr Julian Dodd arrived and pronounced the man dead, which was obvious to all concerned in any case.

"Are you certain it was suicide, Doctor?" Lyons asked as Dodd stood up from examining the corpse.

"Oh, yes, no doubt at all. Classic self-inflicted hanging. Quite common in men of his age," Dodd said in a matter of-fact manner. "Was there a note?"

"Yes, I've taken it as evidence."

"There you are then. Well, you don't need me anymore out here. PM tomorrow at ten." The doctor turned on his heel, got back into his shiny black Lexus and left the scene.

It took Lyons another half an hour to complete the formalities at the scene. The forensic crew had arrived and were taking photographs of every aspect of the site, and the body of Liam McMadden. But there was little evidence to collect, other than the rope. Lyons strolled over to the Ford truck that McMadden owned. She looked in the back, which was open, and saw what looked like two or three short pieces of scaffolding tube. She lifted one out, and put it in another evidence bag. It would be compared to the murder weapon back at the lab, and she had no doubt that a match would be found.

When everyone had finished up, Lyons said to Pascal Brosnan, "Pascal, why don't you drive McMadden's truck back to the hotel car park. The keys are in it. Leave it somewhere a bit out of sight there, and leave the keys with the receptionist."

"Good idea, boss. I'll do that. Are we good to go now?"

"Yes. No point in hanging around. Will Mary be OK?"

"Yes, don't worry, I'll look after her. But she's tougher than you think."

"Good. She'll need to be. You're fond of her, aren't you, Pascal?"

"She's a grand girl, Inspector. We get on well, and we work well as a team."

"That's not quite what I meant," Lyons said, smiling.

"Ah, ye know," Brosnan replied, making no commitment.

"Have you let Séan know about all this?"

"Oh yes, I called him a while back. He's fully up to date."

* * *

Lyons drove back to Roundstone and stopped at the Garda station. Fallon and Fahy were both inside, but the atmosphere was grim.

"Hi, Sally, Mary. Have you been up to the hotel?" Lyons asked.

"Yes, I went and broke the news to Mrs McMadden," Fahy said, "but I got the feeling she already knew. She wanted to know what time he died at. I couldn't tell her, but I said probably sometime yesterday evening, after dark. She's closing the hotel for a few days."

"Did you see Stella?"

"Yes. She was on the desk when I went in, and she heard me telling Mrs McMadden. She was pretty cut up too."

"I can understand that. Well, I suppose I'd better go out and tell the Gilpins. Put them out of their misery. I'll be back in a while, Sally, then we can get back to town."

"Right, boss. Thanks."

Lyons drove back up along Fuchsia Lane to the Gilpins' house. Only Mrs Gilpin was in, and Lyons told her what had transpired, leaving out some of the more difficult details. The woman received the news tearfully, and Lyons had to stay with her for some time to calm her down, but eventually she seemed to accept what she had been told. Her husband would be back in a while, and she assured Lyons that she would be fine till then.

When Lyons and Fahy got back to Mill Street there was a sombre air about the place. No one liked it when a case ended in a further tragedy, as it had this time. They agreed that Liam McMadden was probably not an evil man, just a stupid one, and that although he had killed in anger at his own stupidity, he might well have been rehabilitated had he not elected to end his life by suicide.

The post-mortem confirmed what they all knew, and the case of the murder of Aoife Gilpin was closed.

Epilogue

In the weeks that followed, the Gardaí and Customs and Excise proceeded with their cases against Izzy O'Flaherty, Anthony Miller, Dawid and the crew and captain of the *Paola Marie*. The politicians went quiet when the extent of the smuggling, and the consequential losses to the state's coffers in VAT and excise duty were revealed. Even they found it hard to attempt to defend the indefensible.

The captain of the ship recovered from being shot by Hays, and GSOC absolved Hays of any wrongdoing, reporting that he had acted reasonably given that the man was armed and another officer's life was in danger. The skipper was charged with various offenses, and when he came to court, was given a four-year jail sentence with the last year suspended.

The vessel itself was seized by Customs and was moved out of Galway harbour as it was blocking up the place. It lies rusting in a little-known berth somewhere along the west coast where the sea will eventually deal with it.

Mrs McMadden found it very uncomfortable to stay on as proprietor of the Bertraghboy Bay Hotel. Her business had declined once the full story got out around the village. The locals gave the place a wide berth. The Gardaí formed the impression that she knew a lot more about her husband's dalliances than she let on, but there was little to be achieved in pursuing that line of enquiry, and they were happy that she had nothing to do with his demise. She put the place on the market in January of the following year and achieved a sale in March for a reasonable figure.

The house at Callow was completed by another contractor, and the owners moved in on schedule the following spring. But they moved out again soon afterwards, citing the fact that they felt the property was haunted by the ghost of Liam McMadden. The word got around, and the place could not be sold or rented as a result. It lies empty to this day.

James McMahon was hugely helpful to Séamus and Sheila in negotiating the sale of most of their farmland to their neighbour. As intended, they kept ten acres around the house for themselves, and as soon as the transaction had gone through, Séamus built a piggery and a chicken coop, and stocked it with animals and birds that became almost immediately productive. McMahon sent a fee note to Mick Hays when it was all tied up for €500, which Hays paid promptly and obtained a receipt.

List of Characters

Detective Superintendent Mick Hays – in overall charge of the Galway Detective Unit. A seasoned policeman with loads of experience. As Maureen Lyons' life partner, he admires her occasionally unconventional techniques, but sometimes worries about her safety.

Senior Inspector Maureen Lyons – a feisty detective who is tougher than she seems, but often gets into a tight spot.

Detective Inspector Eamon Flynn – a tenacious member of the team who never lets up until he has his target well and truly cornered.

Detective Sergeant Sally Fahy – a pretty young officer with a keen instinct for identifying a wrongdoer.

Sergeant Séan Mulholland – a wily old officer who runs Clifden Garda station in his own somewhat old-fashioned way. He's addicted to tea and chocolate biscuits.

Garda Pascal Brosnan – the Garda in charge of the small Garda station in Roundstone.

Garda Mary Fallon – lives in Clifden, but has been assigned to Roundstone where she assists Brosnan running the station.

Chief Superintendent Finbarr Plunkett – a wily man who is keen to retain and enhance Galway's excellent reputation for crime detection.

Inspector Niall Griffin – the man in charge of the Armed Response Unit.

Sinéad Loughran – a good-humoured and thorough forensic officer.

Dr Julian Dodd – the state pathologist attached to University Hospital Galway.

James McMahon – a Galway architect who has helped the Gardaí on occasions.

Sheila – Maureen Lyon's sister who runs what was the family farm with her husband near Athenry.

Séamus – Maureen Lyons' brother-in-law.

Aoife Gilpin – a young hotel worker with an interesting sideline.

Izzy O'Flaherty – Aoife's friend who knows more than she lets on.

Gerald Gilpin – Aoife's father.

Brigid Gilpin – Aoife's mother.

Eileen McMadden – runs the Bertraghboy Bay Hotel.

Liam McMadden – Eileen's husband, a builder of sorts.

Stella – works in the Bertraghboy Bay Hotel.

Festus Rourke – an old-timer who tends sheep near Roundstone.

Anthony (Michael) Miller – a smooth operator with a flash car.

Peter – the maître d' at An Béal Bocht.

Mr Wilkinson – a port authority manager.

If you enjoyed this book, please let others know by leaving a quick review on Amazon. Also, if you spot anything untoward in the paperback, get in touch. We strive for the best quality and appreciate reader feedback.

editor@thebookfolks.com

www.thebookfolks.com

MORE BOOKS BY DAVID PEARSON

In this series:

Murder on the Old Bog Road (Book 1)
Murder at the Old Cottage (Book 2)
Murder on the West Coast (Book 3)
Murder at the Pony Show (Book 4)
Murder on Pay Day (Book 5)
Murder in the Air (Book 6)
Murder at the Holiday Home (Book 7)
Murder on the Peninsula (Book 8)
Murder at the Races (Book 9)
Murder in a Safe Haven (Book 10)
Murder in an Irish Bog (Book 11)
Murder in a Seaside Town (Book 12)

In the Dublin Homicides Series:

A Deadly Dividend
A Fatal Liaison
The China Chapter
Lethal in Small Doses
Plane Dead
Passion for Murder

If you have enjoyed David Pearson's Galway Homicides series, check out his series of murder mysteries set in Dublin.

Two very different police officers work together to solve cases in this Irish mystery series with a cozy feel.

For Detective Inspector Aidan Burke, policing Dublin's streets is a duty, but protecting his officers comes first. That provides a good environment for promising detectives like DS Fiona Moore to grow. As this series of murder mysteries set in the metropolitan but at times parochial city and its surroundings progresses, we see Moore tackle difficult and dangerous cases with a good success rate. As Burke himself rises in rank, they become a formidable crime fighting duo.

OTHER TITLES OF INTEREST

Linda Hagan's murder mystery series, set in Belfast.

Meet DCI Gawn Girvin, a detective who gives little away about herself, but one determined to solve the toughest of serious crimes with her sharp mind and steely resolve. Working in one of the roughest cities in the British Isles, she is no stranger to danger. Her cases also take her onto mainland Britain and further afield, tackling incidents that answer to the name of murder. How people react to this fearless Belfast detective is one thing, whether she'll let it affect her is another.

AN EARLY GRAVE
ROBERT McCRACKEN
THE DARING NIGHT
THE SILENT VOICES
ROBERT McCRACKEN
LETHAL DOSE
LETHAL JUSTICE
LETHAL MINDS

Printed in Great Britain
by Amazon

23511338R00118